I0683803

HUNTED

C. R. GARMEN

ALSO BY C.R. GARMEN

TINY TERRORS: HOUSEHOLD HORRORS
ALONG CAME A SPIDER
BECOMING A HERO
HUNTED

HUNTED

C.R. GARMEN

Hunted © C.R. Garmen 2021

All rights reserved. No part of this book may be used or reproduced in any written, electronic, recorded, or photocopied format without the express permission from the author or publisher as allowed under the terms and conditions with which it was purchased or as strictly permitted by applicable copyright law. Any unauthorized distribution, circulation or use of this text may be a direct infringement of the author's rights, and those responsible may be liable in law accordingly. Thank you for respecting the work of this author.

This is a work of fiction. All names, characters, events and places found therein are either from the author's imagination or used fictitiously. Any similarity to persons alive or dead, actual events, locations, or organizations is entirely coincidental and not intended by the author.

COVER AND INTERIOR BY RMGraphX

ACKNOWLEDGEMENTS

Thank you to everyone who has helped me bring this book to life. I would list you all by name, but that would be a book within itself. I'm truly blessed to have such a large and encouraging support system both in person and online. I can't tell you all how much it touches my heart, and how much I appreciate that push you all give for me to follow my dreams. Without you all, this may never have happened.

To my editor, Michael- thank you for being able to guess what I was trying to say. You went above and beyond while dealing with my dyslexic mistakes. That couldn't have been easy. You're amazing.

Special shout out to my fur and fin babies for being extra adorable.

CHAPTER ONE

REY RAMSEY leaned closer to the computer screen, running a hand through his short black hair. He had been here every night after work for the past week, scrolling through ads and comparing prices on homes within Pontiac City, but so far, the numbers didn't run in his favor. Now, he looked outside of the big city and lo and behold, found a place that fit within their budget.

"That's an hour away from the company building," Felicia Ramsey, his beautiful and supportive wife, murmured from over his shoulder. She was almost a foot shorter than him at five-three with a curved body that fit perfectly in his arms. Her long brown hair tickled the side of his neck. He looked back with a small smile.

"True, but it's still better than the two-and-a-half-hour drive it would take to get there from here."

Which was why they both huddled together and

looked over the pictures posted in the forum with a pros and cons list. Currently they rented a two-bedroom apartment in the suburbs. It was great for Sierra, but the place was becoming cramped as she grew older. When Rey was handed a promotion with a heavy raise attached, he couldn't believe his luck. They could finally look into owning a house! But in order to accept the promotion he had to be transferred further away to the corporate building upstate.

"Sierra can't start school until next year anyway, now's the time to do something like this."

"It'll still be a huge adjustment for her," Felicia murmured.

Rey shrugged. "At this point, anywhere we go will be a huge adjustment for her. Besides, small towns are typically safer than larger cities—she'll be taken care of and create lifelong friendships."

"But the drive to school will take half an hour from that one, and we only have one car."

"By then we'll have enough money for a second car. I could finally get that truck I've always wanted," Rey teased.

The hushed conversation went back and forth with notes scribbled sloppily on a bright yellow pad.

"Three bedrooms, two bathrooms. You can make the extra room into an office for your writing."

"Don't wolves live out there? Or bears?"

"I can teach you how to shoot if it'll make you feel better."

"Rey!"

"What? A gun isn't a bad idea regardless of where we live, ya know. And I used to go shooting a lot back in college . . ."

Wrapped up in their own little world, the couple missed the small patter of little feet on the tiled floor. Sierra, dressed in a long, pink nightdress, stood in the living room entry with her teddy bear clutched tightly in her hands. She took mostly after her mom with long, brown hair that had been braided back and was mussed from sleep. Her face was rounded with a tiny button nose, faint natural blush highlighting her chubby cheeks, and thick eyelashes. Her large, blue eyes belonged to her father and blinked in confusion before she finally walked up to Felicia and tugged on her green shirt for attention.

"Where are the bears?" she asked.

Felicia leaned down and scooped her daughter up, holding her close as she scowled at Rey. "Nowhere, baby. Why are you awake?"

Sierra nibbled on her bottom lip as she eyed the monitor on their small, wooden desk. A picture of bright green trees holding up a well-loved tire swing filled the computer screen. It looked pretty, but she didn't understand what it had to do with bears coming after them.

"I had another bad dream . . ." she mumbled.

"Oh honey," Felicia cooed as rubbed the back of the five-year-old in her arms. "I'm sorry about that. Want

3

to talk about it?"

Sierra shook her head and buried it in the crook of her mom's neck.

"Mr. Bunny said it wasn't real. But it felt real to me," she said with a sniff.

"Mr. Bunny is smart. I know it felt really bad, honey, but he is right. The bad dream isn't real. Nothing bad is going to happen, I promise."

Rey nodded in agreement, swiveling around in the chair to stroke his daughter's arm.

"Exactly. You have your mom, and dad, and all of your stuffed animals to protect you. We aren't going to let anything happen to you," he added.

Sierra nodded, slowly drawing back to look at the computer screen again.

"What's that?" she asked, pointing to the picture of an open yard.

Felicia looked at the monitor. "We're looking at pictures of houses."

"Why?"

The two adults exchanged a look before Rey replied, "Well, Daddy got a promotion, but it's too far from where we live now. So, we're going to move somewhere closer."

"It's like a brand-new adventure. It's going to be a lot of fun, you'll love it!" Felicia added with a smile.

Sierra wasn't convinced but watched as her dad clicked on some pictures of different houses with large yards. One had red bricks with a long porch and a brightly colored pot of flowers set out. Another was tall, painted light blue with lots of windows on it. The one made out of logs was funny. She hadn't seen a house like that before.

"We haven't picked one yet. Tell you what, how about in the morning we have pancakes with chocolate chips, and we can all look through these pictures together?" Rey offered with a warm smile.

"What about the bears?"

Rey rolled his eyes. "There aren't going to be any bears. But we'll be able to paint your room any color you want! And you could have a bike! That will be fun. And maybe your own club house. ATVs . . ."

Felicia scowled at him, making him give Sierra a sheepish grin.

"Okay, maybe not ATVs . . . yet," he added with a wink.

Sierra giggled as her mom looked up at a ceiling and mumbled, "Lord help me," under her breath.

"For now, it's time to go back to bed," Felicia stated, rocking her daughter gently before turning towards the small bedroom.

"This will be great, baby. I promise"

CHAPTER TWO

"IN THREE hundred feet, turn left onto Horton Drive," the GPS chirped.

The trees flew by the vehicle as Rey navigated the curves of the road to Fayeville, a small town in the middle of the dense and beautiful forests of Michigan. Felicia sat in the passenger seat, offering him a small smile with her long brown hair twisted up in a bun on the top of her head. He reached over and squeezed her slender hand for support before he returned it to the wheel. The drive wasn't too long, only an hour and a half from their old apartment. It had taken nearly six months to finalize everything and start moving into the house. The bedrooms had been painted two weeks ago, and the movers had gotten the bulk of their belongings inside just the day before.

Driving back and forth had been a hassle, but Sierra was thrilled to learn that each time Mommy and Daddy needed to go set everything up, she got to spend the time with Grandma— who spoiled her constantly.

"What's on your mind?" Rey asked as Felicia stared out the side window.

She shrugged, watching the small buildings in town pop up over the hill.

"I guess I'm worried about how Sierra will take this. She's so young and hasn't been this far away from the city before."

Rey sighed heavily. "Honey, we've had this conversation before. It's for the best. This will make the commute to work easier, and Sierra is going to love having a big bedroom to herself, with a giant backyard to explore."

"Yeah, I know," Felicia murmured, watching the trees and thick, lush bushes pass by. It looked wild and untamed, but that was part of what drew her to this particular town. It had a wild beauty to it that she had never seen before.

The car slowed at the corner, the brick and mortar shops turning into pure forests dotted with small homes of all different designs. A whitewashed one stood out starkly against its green and brown surroundings. A large wooden sign planted in the middle of the lawn painted white with bold black letters that announced, "IT is coming! Be prepared!"

"Are they talking about Jesus or someone else?" she mused.

Rey peeked over at the yard before easing the car

forward as the light changed.

"I can't image who else they would be referring to."

"Cthulhu?"

Rey barked a laugh. "Yeah, okay."

She chuckled and shrugged; her bright green eyes lit up with mischief.

"Hey, you never know!"

Rey just shook his head. "I suppose."

One more turn down a side street and the GPS announced their arrival. The house was hidden from the main road with a curving dirt driveway that wound through the large, looming trees. The bumps and dips were unpleasant to ride over, and the sharp turns forced Rey to crawl forward to avoid hitting any stumps or large arching roots.

The house was a massive two-story cabin and made from thick, gleaming logs. The front porch had artfully curved branches to help guide visitors up the hand-carved steps. A small swing was set up off to the right side of the porch in front of the bay window of the living-room. A tiny garden on either side of the stairs was planted with blooming poppies and buttercups.

The dirt road opened to a large U-shaped drive with a flagpole planted in the center. The driveway had an additional drive that broke off from the front of the house and led off to the side where the parking garage, and a small rundown barn, were built.

Rey parked at the front, turning off the vehicle as his wife unbuckled her seatbelt and climbed out of the car. The doors closed behind them, breaking the quiet of the late afternoon. Their feet crunched over the dirt and leaves on the ground as they approached their new future. Their first home. Their forever home—if everything went right.

Felicia dug the key out of her purple coat pocket as they approached the thick, front door. She slid it into the lock and twisted the knob, opening the door up to the large open living room with an empty stone fireplace, a short gray couch, and a mountain of boxes blocking the view of the glass doors that led to the wide deck and expansive backyard.

To the left, at the edge of the living room, running along the wall was a staircase with smooth branches for a rail that led upstairs to a large office area. A hallway separated the living space from the kitchen area which guided them to the bedrooms in the back of the house. The kitchen was attached to the living room floor plan, with beautiful dark marbled countertops, an island to sit at with stools left by the old homeowners, and a small back hall that took them to the tiny laundry room.

Under the stairway leading up towards the second floor, stood a white door for the attached garage with a small worn-out welcome mat.

"So, where do you want to start?" Rey asked as he approached the looming stack of boxes marked with simple descriptions of where the items inside belonged.

Felicia sighed and said, "Might as well just grab a box and put it in the right room. Then we can put it all away from there."

Rey nodded and grabbed the closest box marked *Sierra's room* and moved towards the hall.

"I feel like packing was easier than this," he remarked before disappearing to their daughter's newly painted room.

Felicia silently agreed as she picked out a box for the kitchen and moved it over to the island. It was going to take forever to get everything ready. But it was worth it. They had been dreaming about owning their own place since before they'd gotten married. It was everything she had wanted, and more. The house was gorgeous, and it was right outside of the town. The next city was only half an hour away if they wanted to visit the mall or go to the movies.

It was perfect.

She grabbed another box and towed it to the laundry room with the washer and dryer combo. A tiny window from over the small counter by the appliances gave her a wonderful view of the back with the line of trees that still bloomed with bright green leaves and wildflowers sprinkled around the grass. A cardinal chirped as it flew past the glass, its vibrant wings spread wide to ride the breeze.

She sighed, placing the box down and leaning closer to the window.

"We should get a birdfeeder," she mused as a flash of brown darted through the thick trunks and foliage.

Felicia blinked, moving closer to the window to try

and see the creature winding through the back more clearly. A flash of a long tail peeking over the bushes for a moment before disappearing from view.

"What on earth?"

Was that a dog? The tail had curved upwards and she swore she had seen a muzzle on the quick glimpse of it's face. But something was off about it. It was dark brown with touches of black. But it moved so fast! She leaned back with a frown. It wasn't a wolf, right?

She shook her head, wolves were smaller. This thing was the size of a Great Dane, maybe bigger, bulkier. It was hard to judge properly from so far away. Perhaps she was overthinking it. They had neighbors, after all. One of them could have a Mastiff, or something, running around.

"Felicia, honey, where do you want this one?"

She rubbed her eyes and turned back to the living room.

"What?"

Rey stood by the couch with a box marked *Christmas stuff* on the side. He paused at the sight of her and cocked his brow.

"Are you all good?"

She shook her head. "Yeah. I think I saw a dog run through the back."

"So? Maybe one of the neighbor's got out or something. Lots of people have dogs around here. Heck, with this much space we could have one too."

Felicia frowned. "I guess . . . I just don't like it

running around when Sierra is going to be here. I don't know if their dogs are friendly. What if one of them bites her?"

"Well, I don't think Sierra is going to be outside by herself much. But, how about we go see the neighbors before we leave? We can get a feel for the people and see if any of them might have aggressive dogs."

"I suppose so . . ."

Rey nodded. "Good. Now, where are we putting these boxes for now?"

Felicia nibbled her bottom lip as she surveyed the room again.

"Maybe we can put them by the front door . . . The garage? No, I don't want them to get damaged by the weather," she muttered to herself. "Isn't there an attic here? We can put them up there for now."

"Sounds good to me. Want to hold the ladder for me?"

"Sure, lead the way."

CHAPTER THREE

THE ATTIC was through the office, in the ceiling by the far-right corner of the room. The wooden trap door was surprisingly large and came down with a metal ladder free of rust or wear, which slid into place with a gentle tug. Rey had pointed it out when they were painting the office, but they had yet to go into it. Why bother when it was barely going to get any use?

Of course, they had forgotten about storing the seasonal décor away.

"What if there are mice up there?" Felicia mused with the box in her arms as her husband placed his foot on the bottom rung of the ladder.

He rolled his eyes at her and took a step up. "There aren't any critters running around in the attic. We had pest control spray the whole house before painting it, remember?"

"Okay, so what if there are dead mice up there?" she

amended with a quirk of her lips.

Rey huffed a laughed, grabbing onto the lip of the attic.

"I'll take a look really quick and let you know. Maybe I'll hide one under your pillow tonight."

"Do it and you'll die. A very long and painful death," she growled as he pulled himself through the hole. His laughter rang down to her as he disappeared from view, making her shift to try and see him.

His boots thudded dully above her as he moved around.

Thump, thump, thump.

Pause.

Thump, thump, thump.

"Honey, you have to see this!" he announced in awe, popping his head back through the doorway. "You're going to love it!"

Felicia carefully handed up the box of Christmas items before grabbing onto the ladder. She tested the first rung, biting her bottom lip nervously. But it held and stayed firmly in place as she moved up to the doorway.

Rey moved back as she pulled herself inside with a grunt. The thick layer of dust on the floor stirred as she stumbled up to her feet. Light shone in through a single window behind them, illuminating the empty space covered in dust, dirt, and cobwebs. Rey reached out to hold her steady as Felicia got her bearings and turned around to see what had her husband so excited.

In the very back where the tiny window resided, sat a large desk with a dollhouse resting on top. The peak of the wooden structure obscured some of the light, casting long shadows at their feet and hiding the design of the desk from their view. Still, it was breathtaking in its well-worn glory, hiding as a lost treasure under years of accumulated dust.

"Wow, how old is that desk?"

The awe in her voice made Rey smile and shrug. "It needs to be cleaned off before I could even guess. But it looks pretty old."

Her hands fluttered around the drawers with ornament handles with locks that probably no longer had a proper key, before moving to inspect the house on top. It took her breath away. Small wooden logs decorated the outside, a few looked ready to fall off but could easily be hot glued back into place. The small rooms inside replicated their house perfectly, save for the wallpaper. There were four nondescript almost peg-looking wooden dolls inside. Two were middle height with one tall and one small standing in the attic of the dollhouse. A tiny wooden couch that needed to be repainted rested in the living room, and little wooden beds had been left in each of the bedrooms.

"I can't believe this was left behind. The craftsmanship is absolutely amazing." Felicia paused with a growing smile as she turned to face her husband. "Sierra would love this!"

"Their loss is our gain," Rey said with a lazy smile,

"and that's what I thought when I saw it. We could use it to help her adjust to the new house."

Felicia nodded. "I could make those dolls look like all of us. Oh, it will be so cute! I just need to clean it up, change some of the rooms. Get some more tiny furniture perhaps . . ."

Rey wrapped his arms around her, resting his head on her shoulder.

"I know you'll make it perfect. And we can put it in her new room to surprise her with when we officially move in."

She placed her hand on top of his arms and leaned into his body.

"Well, you know what this means," she mused.

"Huh?"

"If we want to finish moving by next week, I'll have to start working on this dollhouse now and leave the unpack to you," she said with a wicked smile.

Rey tilted his head down to look at her, his eyes dancing with humor. "Oh, is that what this mean?"

"Absolutely!"

He chuckled, kissing her forehead before letting her go and stepping back with a sigh.

"And I guess you'll need to go into town for craft supplies while I stay here, sweating and bleeding from all of these boxes?" he added, placing a hand over his heart with a pout.

She rolled her eyes and nodded. "Yep! Good luck, baby. I'll be cheering for you while I paint!"

"Well, since you're going into town, want to grab some burgers for lunch?" he asked while fishing the car keys and wallet from his pocket.

She chuckled, grabbing the items he offered to her and tucking them away. "Sure. That sounds good to me. I'll probably be about an hour, though."

"That's fine, it'll give me time to unbury your crafting stuff," he said, putting his hands in his pockets. "Thank goodness we have all weekend to get this done. We have a lot to do."

Felicia nodded, giving him a cheeky grin as she lowered herself through the trapdoor.

"Yes, we do, so you had better get started!"

He laughed, following her out.

"Yeah, I guess I should—hey, make my burger a large combo!"

"No problem, baby. I love you," she purred.

"I love you, too, sweetheart."

Rey watched his wife carefully lower herself down to the empty office space before turning back to the desk. The dollhouse was a beautiful and mysterious gift. Maybe it would help, he mused as he inspected the dusty interior once more. Or maybe it wouldn't . . .

But they certainly would embrace it along with their new life. The blessings that had been offered to him were more than he could thank any being in existence for. It was a dream come true and so much more.

Rey walked around the desk, the cramped space making him duck his head as he used the light of the sun to judge how much work would need to go into fixing the house up. The logs were cracked in some places, and peeling off in others, but it wasn't bad for a child's toy. Obviously, it had been well-loved. His shoe slipped on something as he pushed away from the back wall. He frowned as he moved back and bent down to the floor to scoop up a torn, yellow piece of paper. In the limited rays of the sunlight he could barely make out the fading ink scrawled across the page.

Rey moved around the front of the desk and tilted the paper back and forth curiously. There was a smudge near the top corner—a date perhaps? It was too difficult to tell for certain. The rest of the writing was long and looping with a feminine curve to the etched letters.

Man lived with dirt until dirt became mud. One hundred and ten and seven and so two became one.

He frowned, flipping the page over, but the back was blank. He turned it back over and reread the short message. It didn't make any sense to him, but it didn't belong to him, so obviously it wouldn't. He shrugged, stuffing the paper into his pocket with a mental note to throw it away once he got back downstairs.

His boots thudded on the floorboards as he crossed the room for the open door. As he peered down at the ladder, a thought made him jerk back and groan.

"Shit, I think we forgot to bring trash bags."

CHAPTER FOUR

"**ARE YOU** excited to have a big girl bedroom, honey?" she asked.

Sierra shrugged in response, picking at a loose string on her yellow blouse. The car was stuffed with the items they couldn't move until they finally left the apartment for good. Boxes and bags with their blankets and pillows took up the trunk, with most of the stuffed animals she told her parents she couldn't possibly sleep without. Not even for a day.

But they couldn't bring her friends from daycare along. Or her dance class. Sierra was promised they would look into other activities to join at the new home, but it wasn't the same. Nothing was going to be the same anymore.

"What about the big backyard? You'll have tons of space to run outside and play with your friends," Rey added.

Again, Sierra just shrugged. Her friends were back home, she didn't understand how leaving them so far behind was something she was supposed to be excited about. Almost as if her mother could read her mind—and Sierra was pretty sure she could—she said, "You'll make a lot of new friends in our new home, honey. And we can always call up your old friends like Maisy and Amber for a sleepover on the weekends."

Sierra sighed and nodded in agreement before turning to look out the window again. They were heading into the small town with dozens of tiny stores pressed together in long strips on the main road. Train tracks crisscrossed through the streets, rattling the car and everything inside of it. It looked nice, she supposed. It was better than the pictures she had seen.

"Just give it a chance, Sierra. I'm sure you'll love it here," her dad said quietly.

She wasn't convinced, but the move was already done. The U-Hauls with all their furniture and belongings had already arrived the week before. Felicia and Rey had sent Sierra to her grandma's to sort their things into the right rooms and begin unpacking boxes.

The move was supposed to be better for her daddy. He had received a promotion at work and was transferred further out with it. Her parents told her that it meant a lot of new and better things would happen for their family. Sierra could have a brand-new bike for her birthday and maybe a playhouse in the backyard. But it didn't feel like she was getting any new gifts. It felt like she was losing everything she knew.

"Can I still see Nana?" Sierra suddenly asked, her voice squeaking as they rolled over another set of train tracks.

"Of course! Nana will visit us, and you can go over to her house on the weekends," Felicia assured her.

"You can still see and talk to everyone you want, it's just a little bit further of a drive now. It's not that big of a deal," Rey added. "We're just moving away to have more space, and so Daddy doesn't have to drive two hours to work every day. You still want to see Daddy before bedtime, right? If we stayed at the apartment, I might not have been able to see you every night."

Sierra fidgeted in her seat. "I want to see you before bed," she stated quietly.

"That's why we're moving, pumpkin. Everything is going to be great, I promise you."

"Okay," Sierra sighed, but still . . . she wasn't convinced.

"Your destination is coming up on the left," the GPS announced.

Sierra sat up higher to look out the window at the winding dirt driveway that bounced the car a lot. It was long and eventually turned into cement by the big house with flowers blooming in small gardens. It even had a little garden gnome standing straight up with a big, pointy red hat to guard it.

Rey grinned as he pulled up front and parked the car. He clapped his hands together and twisted in his seat to look at his daughter.

"Are you ready to take a look inside your new home?" he asked.

Sierra nodded and unbuckled her seatbelt. Her mother was outside of the car before she had time to open up her own door, with her father following shortly behind her.

"Welcome home, honey!" Felicia exclaimed as she scooped Sierra into her arms. "We picked the biggest room just for you."

Sierra grabbed a faded pink plushy of a rabbit with long floppy ears, and black beaded eyes. Mr. Bunny being one of her favorite well-worn stuffed animals, went with her everywhere.

"We even have your bedroom set up and ready to go for you and all of your toys."

She would need to talk to Mr. Bunny about how his night went. Maybe the new house wouldn't be that bad. But if Mr. Bunny had nightmares, then she needed to convince her parents to take them back. Mr. Bunny was smart, Sierra trusted him to be a good judge of wise moves.

"And we have a big surprise for you, too," her daddy teased.

Sierra perked up a little. "What kind of surprise?"

Felicia unlocked the front door and pushed it open. "You'll have to go and see," she added with a wink back at Rey. Sierra looked around the living room with their gray couch sitting in the middle of the hardwood floors and flat screen TV hanging above a large fireplace. Side tables were placed at the ends of the couch with family photos resting on them. A low coffee table sat a few feet in front of the couch with some books resting on top and coasters for their cups. It looked warm and cozy, even if it was new.

Down the hallway, the first door on the left belonged to Sierra's new room. Her parents stood on either side of the wood trim around the entrance, Rey's hand on the polished golden handle with eager and nervous smiles on their faces. Rey twisted the knob and, after few vague teases about what was inside, finally pushed opened it up and to let Sierra step inside.

Pink! Everything was pink! The room was a lot larger than her one back at the apartment, with pastel pink walls decorated with pictures of rainbows and rabbits. It had a big window, with tons of floor space and a closet that took up almost the entire side wall.

Her bed was pushed by the window with a thin, pink curtain surrounding the mattress to give her a princess tent inside. Her small desk was set up with all her art supplies laid out on top, and a new plushy pillow was placed on the small red plastic chair.

But what made her gasp and squeal in excitement was the dollhouse in the middle of the floor on a bright pink rug. It looked exactly like the house they had just moved into! Logs decorated the outside, and in it had wallpaper to match the color of the bedrooms and living area.

Felicia laughed and set her down so Sierra could inspect the tiny house further. The details were perfect, down to the granite countertops in their kitchen and the floral designed curtains in the windows.

"Do you like it?" Rey asked while she bounced around the replica clapping her hands.

"It's so pretty! And it's so big! Much bigger than my old dollhouse!"

"The old homeowners left it behind, so we fixed it up for you. And I made these to go along with it," her mommy explained while pulling out three little peg dolls.

Sierra took the dolls and carefully turned them in her hands to inspect them. The tallest doll had short black hair and blue eyes like her dad, with a copy of his favorite flannel shirt on. The second doll looked like her mom with long brown hair and green eyes, and a long red dress. The smallest was a replica of herself with the brown hair pulled back into a ponytail, blue eyes, and a yellow blouse on just like the one she was wearing.

Sierra beamed up at her parents, clutching the small toys to her chest.

"Thank you, Mommy and Daddy!"

Her dad reached down to ruffle her hair. "Of course, pumpkin. Why don't you go ahead and play with your new toys while I finish unloading the car and Mommy starts dinner?"

Her mom gave her forehead a quick kiss before

striding out the door. "And if you need anything, just call us."

"Okay!"

CHAPTER FIVE

REY CAREFULLY set down another box from the car while Felicia diced onions in the kitchen. He placed his hands on her hips and surveyed the arrangement of chopped vegetables.

"Do you think you'll be ready to go to work on Monday?" Felicia asked, leaning back into him.

Rey sighed, placing a quick kiss on her cheek. "I hope so. This promotion is so amazing, I couldn't turn it down. I just hope it lives up to the hype my boss has been giving it."

Felicia placed her knife aside and turned to face him in his arms.

"And you deserve it. You've been with this company for almost fifteen years. I'm sure everything will be fine. And if not, money isn't everything."

He smiled down at her. "No, but it's nice. This is going to give us enough financially that we won't have to carefully budget every week for the bills. Or groceries. In fact, we could think about expanding our family a little more . . ." he offered with a wicked grin.

Felicia blushed and giggled. "I thought we were going to wait to get settled in before talking about that."

He waved a hand around dismissively. "We're almost done. We only need to unpack what we brought along . . . We could send Sierra to your mom's next weekend."

Felicia swatted his side playfully, her eyes lit up with that hungry gleam he loved. Her hair was pulled back into a messed bun with curling strands escaping the ponytail holder and falling around her heart-shaped face. She licked her lips, pulling away and turning her gaze out the back door.

"Oh wow, look at all of those deer!" she gasped, drawing him out of the moment to peer at the group of fawn nibbling on their yard.

"You don't get to see something like this out in the city," he murmured.

Felicia muttered an agreement, counting the herd grazing quietly. "There must be about twenty of them out there," she whispered.

"Should we go get Sierra?"

Rey thought about it for a moment before shrugging. "Let her keep playing in her room. I'm sure we'll see this a lot while we're living here."

"Oh, I forgot! We should get a bird feeder! She'll love watching the robins and blue jays eating every day."

"Of course, and we can build a firepit to roast marshmallows in the evenings before bed," Rey added.

"This is perfect, my love. You did an amazing job finding this home," Felicia praised with another kiss on his cheek.

Rey blushed faintly. "It wasn't all me. I just found the place, you're the one that made everything happen."

Felicia chuckled. "We make a great team."

"That we do. I love you so much."

"And I love you."

Felicia turned back to her work on the counter, scooping the onion up and adding it to a bowl before placing a mushroom on the cutting board.

"So, what do you want to do with that desk upstairs?"

"Huh?" Rey reached over quickly, grabbed a slice of pepper and popped it into his mouth.

"In the attic, that desk—remember? I have it cleaned off, but what are we going to do with it?"

"Oh." Rey licked his lips as he eyed another piece. Felicia paused cutting and narrowed her eyes at him, pointing the blade towards him as he went to reach for another. He chuckled and drew his hand back slowly.

"I don't know. What do you want to do with it?"

She watched him for a moment longer before returning to slicing the mushroom with a shrug.

"I don't know. We could always sell it. Or move it into the office. I just hate thinking about it sitting around unused for years again. It's so pretty, it deserves to be seen."

"Honestly," Rey began as he settled onto one of the stools. "I agree with you, but I'm not looking forwards to moving that thing. It's big and heavy."

Her lips quirked up. "I know, and I feel bad asking you to do it, but tell me that it wouldn't look great as a computer desk or something. And I could always help you move it."

He snorted and snagged another pepper when she paused to look up at him.

"What is that supposed to mean? And stop stealing the peppers! I won't have any to finish cooking!" she scolded.

Rey swallowed and licked his lips. "It was only two pieces, that's hardly going to ruin the meal. And I just mean that you have a hard time lifting a full jar of pickles. No offense, but how are you going to help me pick up an antique desk?"

She rolled her eyes and said, "First, I do not struggle lifting a jar of pickles. Second, do you really think it's an antique?"

"Looks old as hell, so I would wager so," he mused with a shrug.

"And I'm not saying I won't move it," Rey added, pointedly ignoring her assertion. "I'm just saying it won't be fun. And I probably won't move it twice so you gotta figure out where it's going because it'll be staying there for a few years."

"Fine," she huffed, turning away to move a skillet onto the front burner of the stove.

"I'll do some research on it and let you know. If it really is an antique, we should keep it and then sell it closer to when Sierra is getting ready for college."

"Why wait until then?"

"I'm hoping it'll increase in value the longer we hold onto it. College is going to cost an arm and a leg. We'll need every edge we can get preparing for it."

Rey rolled his eyes but smiled. "Fine. Let me know when you figure this out."

She peered over her shoulder and stuck her tongue out at him.

"Oh, trust me, I will."

Rey stared straight at her as he snagged another pepper and tossed it into his mouth.

"Great, I'm looking forward to it."

CHAPTER SIX

SIERRA GUIDED her dolls to the living room and set everyone down on the gray couch in front of the fireplace. It was almost time for bed, so the family was going to read together. It was her favorite way to end the day. Especially when Daddy pulled out the big princess book and read her "Cinderella."

"Once upon a time . . ."

A sound startled Sierra from her story. She looked wildly around her room but nothing looked out of place. The sound came again, this time from her closet. Slowly, Sierra climbed to her feet and made her way over to the large sliding doors. She took a calming breath and slid the wooden panel back. Inside the closet were shelves with books, clothing, and dolls that she didn't play with as often anymore. She pushed some hangers aside to stare at the blank wall in the back but nothing looked like it had fallen or was out of place.

With a frown, Sierra stepped back and slowly closed the doors again.

Another knock tapped against the door, making Sierra jump. She yanked the door back open to see a figurine on the shelf with her old dolls and playthings. It looked like a dog standing on its hindlegs with its back hunched, and long, sharp claws reaching out for her. She yelped and fell backwards.

"*Mommy!*" she cried, scrambling back up to her feet and bolting from her room. "*Mommy!*"

Felicia nearly dropped the pan of chicken tenders when her daughter blew into the kitchen. She placed the food aside and fell to her knees, gathering her daughter into her arms.

"There's a monster in my closet!" Sierra wailed.

Felicia cooed and rocked her gently, trying to calm the five-year-old down before addressing the concern. "What monster, honey?"

"It's a doll, and it looks like a monster, and it's in my closet!" she continued to cry.

"Okay, okay, let me go take a look at it. I'm sure everything is fine."

Sierra sniffed and stepped back so her mom could stand back up. Everything would be fine, because Mom and Dad always got rid of anything spooky and nasty in her room. The ugly doll didn't stand a chance.

They walked together, hand in hand, back to the bedroom with toys scattered across the floor. The closet door was shut, making Sierra stop and tug her mom back towards the hall.

"He closed the door! We have to leave!" she begged.

Her mom barely suppressed an eyeroll as she gently untangled her hand from her daughter's squeezing grip. "A doll can't close or open doors," she stated simply.

"No, I know I left it open!"

Felicia sighed, placing her hand on the bright yellow knob. "You probably yanked on it too hard, and it bounced closed after you ran from the room. You have to be careful, honey, the door is on a set of wheels and could pop off the track very easy. I don't want you getting hurt in here," she explained patiently as she slid back the door.

Sierra closed her eyes as her mom inspected the closet from top to bottom. The seconds ticked back quietly, making a knot grow in her stomach.

"Sierra come take a look. There is nothing here," Felicia called.

The little girl opened an eye, peeking at her mom cautiously. "Where did it go?"

"I think your imagination got the better of you. See? Nothing inside of here except for some of your other toys and clothes."

Sierra approached the closet with a scowl, but her mommy was right. The doll wasn't on the shelf anymore. It was gone.

"But I really saw it!" she insisted, pushing back a rack of dresses.

Her mom just sighed and ruffled her hair. "Well,

there is nothing here anymore. Dinner is almost done, so why don't you go get cleaned up, okay?"

Sierra bit her bottom lip and nodded. "Okay."

"Good, I want you at that table in ten minutes," Felicia added as she walked out of the room. "So, no more playing, all right?"

"I will be there!" Sierra promised, slowly pulling herself away from the closet. Was Mommy, right? Did she just imagine it? She couldn't have. It was real. But where did it go?

Sierra closed the door and waited a moment before yanking it back open. Nothing, again. Under the bed, perhaps? She frowned as she turned around to eye her room suspiciously. If the monster was playing hide-and-seek then he was very good at it.

She checked her desk drawers, under the bed, behind her pillows, inside the dollhouse, and inside the closet yet again. It was nowhere to be seen.

"I guess Mommy scared it away," she mumbled, heading out to the bathroom to wash her hands like she promised. That was good. That was what she wanted. So why was she still afraid to go back to her room?

"Hurry up, Sierra, baby!" her dad called.

Sierra turned off the faucet and dried her hands while yelling back that she would be there in a moment.

It was just her imagination. The monster wasn't real. It wasn't coming back.

When Sierra walked up to the small round dinner table, her parents were already there making up the plates. The food was steaming and made her mouth water. Her mother helped her into a chair and together they said grace before digging into the hot potatoes and chicken.

Her parents discussed what still needed to be put away and cleaned in the house. It didn't interest Sierra until Rey started talking about the big forest in the backyard with a duck blind in it.

"What's a duck blind?"

"It's a tiny hide for hunters to use while they are trying to catch animals," he answered. "But you shouldn't go inside of it until I can check it out. The building might not be good anymore."

"Yeah, and there's a lot of animals outside, so I want you stick close to the house until we get a better feel for our land. If you hear anything, or see a raccoon or something approach you, don't try and touch it! Back away and come inside, okay?" Felicia added.

Sierra nodded and poked at her mashed potatoes. "What kind of animals are back there?"

Rey paused in thought and shared a look with his wife that Sierra couldn't decipher.

"Raccoons, possums, rats, maybe some coyotes. Just be careful, okay?"

"I will," Sierra promised.

"Good."

CHAPTER SEVEN

SIERRA WOKE up to a faint howl outside of the house. The sound was far off, but she pulled her thick quilt up to her chin to keep herself safe regardless. It was eerie, echoing off of the branches that creaked in the wind. The bathroom light had been left on, leaving a soft yellow glow under her bedroom door. But beyond that everything was cast in a deep shadow.

The vague shapes of her dollhouse and toys on the floor looked more sinister than mere hours ago when the room was filled with the soft golden light that her father read to her under. Clothing that she had forgotten to put in the hamper were now puddles of ink on the wooden floorboards. She was five, she was a big girl now. None of these things were alive, nor would a hand reach out from under the bed to grab her ankles.

Still, she pulled the blanket higher to her mouth and squeezed her eyes closed. Falling back to sleep was much harder than going to sleep in the first place. The constant gust of wind that rattled her windowsill was distracting. Those howls in the distance sent shivers down her spine. Chirps of crickets, fluttering large wings, and creaking from somewhere nearby made her mind buzz with the possibilities of what was wandering around outside. Or inside.

One creak in particular made her mouth go dry. It was the soft sound of wheels moving against a plastic track. Sierra prayed silently before daring to look over towards her closet. The door was opened an inch. The monster was back.

Her small body shook as she waited to be attacked. She couldn't manage to release the scream that was building up inside of her. Yet she couldn't just wait to die. She needed to do something. But if she left the safety of her bed, would that make it easier for the beast to find her? Would that spark the chase that would ultimately end her life? What about her mom and dad?

Time slowly moved by, and nothing else happened. Even the howls outside seemed to stop. Only the occasional hoot from an owl assured her that the minutes still ticked by. Everything in her room remained still.

Sierra took a deep breath and threw her blankets back. She sprung up from her bed and dashed across the floor as though it were lava. In a few seconds she reached the light switch and flipped it on as hard as she could, breathing out when the room lit up in that soft, warm glow of light. Blinking to clear her vision, Sierra scanned the floor to find the figurine from before.

The dollhouse and toys were right where she had left them. Except . . . Sierra creeped closer to the house and peeked inside. The little peg dolls weren't on the couch anymore. The two pegs of her parents were lying on a wooden bed in their bedroom. Inside her bedroom, her peg was standing by the light switch.

Her heart raced as she stared in disbelief. When did they move? How did they move? Slowly she turned to face her closet. On the floor two tiny red eyes stared back at her. The clawed arms of the dog-like creature were held out, reaching for her from the doorway.

Sierra screamed.

Thumps of pounding feet raced down the hallway before her bedroom door was thrown open. Her parents rushed in, surrounding her and pulling her into the safety of their arms. But she couldn't stop. The only thing she could do was to point at her closet door. The door that was still cracked open with a monster staring out at the scene unfolding. Her parents were talking but none of their words pierced through the continuous wailing of horror that poured from her throat. Her vision blurred with tears and her lungs gasped for air.

It was her father who finally noticed the figure on the floor and went to retrieve it as her mother bounced her and tried to calm her down.

"What is this?"

Sierra didn't care what it was. It was a monster and it was stalking her. But the tiny toy looked almost innocent in her father's large hands as he turned it this way and that. She felt her mother shrug, and as her screams finally died down to coughs and whimpers, she could hear them mulling over what the creature was, and how it had appeared.

"Maybe another thing left behind by the old homeowners?"

"Who would play with such a thing?" her mother asked, wrinkling her nose in distaste.

Her father shrugged. "Probably a little boy. Or maybe a teenage who was obsessing over some movie or something."

"You think it's from a movie?"

Her dad yawned. "Why not? Looks like something out of a cheesy horror flick. I had a few figures of the swamp creature when I was younger."

"Where did it come from?"

"We probably missed it when we were cleaning out of the closet, and then Sierra knocked it down while she was playing. It doesn't matter, I'm throwing it out, anyway."

Her mother nodded, sitting on the edge of the bed with Sierra pressed tightly to her chest. "Hear that, honey? Daddy is going to take care of it. Everything is all right."

Sierra sniffed and nodded, but the sinking feeling of doubt wouldn't let go.

"Trust me, sweetheart, we'll take care of it. Now, let's get you back to bed," Felicia cooed, carefully laying her daughter back on the mattress.

Rey watched them for a moment before stepping out into the hall with the strange figure in his hand. He closed the door quietly behind him, listening in as Felicia offered to read Sierra another bedtime story. It would be a few minutes before she came back out.

He padded into the kitchen and popped open the lid to the trash can, dropping the creepy toy inside. Rey hesitated, then pulled the bag out of the can. If Sierra woke up in the morning and saw the wolf-like creature when she was throwing away her leftovers, she would have another fit. He slipped on his shoes and stepped out the back door. The wind was cool, but the moon was full and bright, guiding him as he walked out to the garage where they would be storing their trash cans until the city came around to collect them.

The door to the barn squealed as he opened it, making him cringe and promise to grab some lubricant from the store when he went into town. He tossed the bag into the large can and that was it. Rey grinned to himself as he left and trudged back up the slight slope in the yard to the house. No more monster, no more waking up screaming in the middle of the night. The only saving grace was that he wasn't scheduled to work in the morning.

He carefully locked the door behind him and crept back to the bedroom, pausing at Sierra's door to listen to Felicia wrap up a story about the three little pigs. Perfect. Now they could all relax and go back to blissful sleep.

As he stepped into their bedroom and flipped on the lights, another howl split the air. It sounded close by, making him grimace. The only downside to living out in the country was the animals that lurked around after dark. Maybe he should get something to protect everyone with. Bear spray, or a rifle. Something.

The howl died down, and after a few minutes silence fell back around him. As long as they were careful, everything would be all right.

CHAPTER EIGHT

THE NEXT two days passed without incident. Everyone finally finished putting all of their belongings away and were settling into the house well. Rey decided to dig out a firepit, line it with bricks he had found in the barn, in the backyard and collect some branches to have a fire later in the evening, but the herd of deer came back and put his plans on hold. The animals captured his wife's and daughter's hearts as they grazed on the long blades of grass near the edge of the woods.

"Does the group look smaller than last time?" Felicia whispered to him as Sierra snapped a thousand pictures of the deer with his phone.

Rey raised an eyebrow and said, "I suppose it does look like it's short by a few bucks, but that's how it goes out here. Other animals have to eat, too."

Felicia rolled her eyes and watched as Sierra crouched down to get a new angle on the camera lens.

"You don't think we're going to find any carcasses around our house, do you? I don't want Sierra to see that."

Rey shrugged, tucking his hands into his pockets. "I doubt it, but I can go look later to be sure. Besides, that's why we told her to stay close to the house."

"Daddy, look! I got a lot of pictures!" Sierra exclaimed, jumping up with the phone extended to him. Rey took it with a doting smile as he scrolled through the dozens of blurred images on his camera roll.

"Good job, honey. Now we can show Nana what a herd of deer look like," he praised, earning a bright smile from her.

"When is she coming over?" Sierra inquired.

"I think she'll be here next weekend. Are you excited? What are you going to show her first?"

"The deer!" Sierra said with a giggle, "and then my princess bed!"

Felicia smiled. "I'm sure she will love those. I'm going to start dinner; do you want to help me?"

Sierra nibbled on her bottom lip for a moment before shaking her head. "Can I go play?"

"Sure thing, honey. Have fun," Felicia encouraged, making her daughter smile again and bounce off to her bedroom.

"Do you want me to help?" Rey offered.

Felicia laughed. "Sure thing, thank you. You can chop the carrots for the soup."

Sierra closed her door on the giggles of her mother

as her parents started dinner. She spun around to greet Mr. Bunny and Pepper the Pig. Skipping up to her dollhouse, she plopped down in front of it to continue the adventure she had started earlier in the morning. Mommy doll was just about to take Sierra doll to the toy store while Daddy doll was at work. But when she peeked inside the house, none of the dolls were where she had left them last.

Mommy doll and Daddy doll were standing in the kitchen by the counter and Sierra doll was standing in the middle of her bedroom.

A creepy feeling crawled up Sierra's arms as she peered around her room again. She bit her bottom lip, wondering if she should call for her parents again. But what would they do? Move the dolls and then tell her that she simply forgot where she had left them again?

"Why are you moving around?" she asked quietly, peering closer at the pegs.

Nobody answered her. She wasn't sure if she was disappointed or relieved. Maybe the dolls were trying to play with her? Maybe it wasn't spooky at all. Maybe this was a good thing. She knew where everyone in the house was. That was kind of cool. Or maybe her parents were right, her imagination was getting the best of her.

Sierra spun away from the dollhouse to grab her pink, plush bunny and pulled him close.

"What happened, Mr. Bunny? Is someone trying to play with us?" she asked him. She turned back to her dollhouse and gasped. The daddy peg was gone, and the mommy peg was now standing in front of the tiny stove.

Something was definitely weird about this. Sierra put her bunny aside while searching inside the dollhouse for the missing figure. It wasn't until she peeked through the clear back doors that she found him standing outside on the pink rug. Her brows scrunched together as she picked the toy up and put him back inside the house. Curiosity pulled at her until she stood up and crept out to the hallway. Her mom's soft humming carried down the hall.

Slowly she inched closer to the living room and popped her head around the corner. Her mom was standing in front of the stove, stirring something inside of a large boiling pot.

"Mommy? Where's Daddy?" she asked quietly, stepping out into the open floor space.

Her mom spun around with a hand to her heart. "I didn't hear you, Sierra, you almost gave me a heart attack!"

"I'm sorry."

Felica laughed nervously and turned back to the pot on the stove. "It's okay, honey, Dad's outside prepping the firepit for the bonfire tonight. Do you need something from him?"

Sierra shook her head. "No, I was just wondering where he was . . ."

Her mom raised a brow. "Okay . . . Well, dinner is

almost done. Go wash up for me, okay?"

"I will," Sierra promised before spinning around and running back into her room.

The dolls were back in their places. Mommy peg was in the kitchen, Daddy peg was outside, and Sierra peg was standing in the middle of her bedroom.

Sierra sat back down in front of the dollhouse and reevaluated it. Nothing looked off. Was this some kind of magic?

"Mommy!" she called. "I need you!"

Sierra kept her eyes on the little dolls while she listened to her mom walk down the hall. The soft thuds of her feet stopped for a moment, then the door swung up.

"Yes? What's going on, Sierra?"

The pegs never moved. Sierra frowned at them and picked the mommy version up again.

"Sierra? Look at me please and tell me what is going on. Why aren't you washing up for dinner?"

Sierra blushed and slowly turned around to face her mom. She couldn't tell her what was happening. She wouldn't believe her, just like she didn't believe the monster doll existed until Dad had found it that night.

She licked her lips and fidgeted in place. "Um, I was going to wash up . . . but I thought I broke my doll."

Her mom sighed. "Well, we can take a look at it after we eat. Now, go clean up, please, and I'll see you at the table in five minutes."

Sierra nodded as her mom left the room, leaving the

door open behind her. She looked back down at the peg in her hand and turned it around carefully.

"What are you doing?" she mumbled.

Her mom called out for her again, and Sierra set the toy back inside the dollhouse living room.

"I'm washing up right now!" she yelled back while scrambling to her feet and running into the bathroom. Whatever was going on, she would have to figure it out later.

CHAPTER NINE

THE BUGS were horrible, and the smoke kept blowing in their faces. Everyone was sitting in plastic folding chairs that Rey had dug out from the garage, but the night wasn't going quite as planned. Felicia waved a hand in front of her face as another breeze blew the thick, eye-burning smoke back into her face. Sierra was scooting her chair away and swatting at the swarm of mosquitos that had invaded their tiny camp. The small bag of marshmallows hadn't been opened yet, nor the crackers and chocolate for s'mores.

Rey sighed as he adjusted his chair to battle the wind. "Maybe we should try this another night," he mused.

Felicia swatted away a fly and nodded in agreement. "Or we should try this earlier in the day? Where did all of these darn bugs come from?"

Sierra frowned, eyeing the poor uneaten treats

lying nearby on a white plastic table. "What about the s'mores?" she whined.

"Sorry, pumpkin, this night is too miserable to roast marshmallows," her dad apologized.

Felicia stood up and collapsed her chair. "How about this? You help us clean up and we'll make some treats inside to eat?"

Sierra smiled and bounced off her chair, pausing the swat again at the swarm of bugs hanging over them. "Okay! Can it have marshmallows in it?"

Rey laughed. "Sure thing. Let's hurry up and get away from these bugs before they drain us dry."

Felicia took the chairs to the garage while Rey put out the fire, and Sierra ran inside with the treats. The crackers were crushed against her chest, but she was pretty sure they would be all right. The back porch light was off, and Sierra wondered briefly if she should turn it on for her mom and dad. Once the fire was out and the smoke was billowing upwards in a thick, high tower, the yard was too dark to see far out in.

She placed the snacks on the kitchen counter and wandered back to the glass doors. She could hear them moving around and talking back and forth to one another, though the words were lost in the distance. Crickets chirped loudly as bats flew low around the deck.

Sierra reached up for the light switch when the first howl ripped through the night. She flinched and then hit the switch as quickly as she could. The backyard lit up, but her parents weren't in sight. Sierra pressed herself against the glass, eyes darting around the shadows of the trees at the edge of the property. The firepit was in the middle of their yard, so where did everyone go?

The howl faded before another started up, sending shivers down her spine.

"Mommy?"

Sierra frowned when nothing outside moved except for the branches in the trees. She turned around and looked at the hallway. Then she looked back outside at the empty yard. Without giving it a second thought, she darted for the hall and turned the corner to her bedroom. She flung the door open hard enough that it bounced off the wall and slowly closed behind her as she flipped on the lights and dashed to the dollhouse.

Sierra peg was inside her bedroom again, but the other dolls were missing. She looked around the outside of the house and couldn't find them. Her heart started to race. Where did they go? Where were her parents?

She looked underneath her bed and under the clothes still strung across her floor from the night before. A soft creaking noise made her freeze. She licked her lips before slowly turning to the closet. The door was cracked open, and the mommy and daddy peg were lying just outside of it. What did it mean?

Sierra crawled across the floor and picked up the pegs, turning them around to make sure they weren't damaged. They looked fine, which was a short-lived feeling of relief. But why weren't they by the house?

She lifted a shaking hand and pulled the closet door open a little further. Standing almost an inch from the door was the wolf-man figurine again. Sierra threw herself back and opened her mouth to scream just as another howl ripped through the air.

"*Mom! Dad!*" Sierra climbed to her feet and slammed the closet door shut on the monster, then spun around and ran into the living room. The porch light was still on, bathing the backyard in a bright golden light. She pressed herself against the glass, staring out into the empty stretch of yard with fear pounding through her veins.

"*Mom! Dad!*"

The garage door opened, and her parents finally emerged. They were still talking to one another as her dad locked the door behind them. Then they strolled across the grass, looking up and waving at her without a care in the world. Her fear subsided some until she heard another howl start.

Her tiny fists knocked on the glass as she jumped and screamed for them to hurry. To run. To get inside before they were eaten. Yet, for some reason, her parents seemed unfazed by the situation. Her mom even paused to look back at the tree line before she shrugged and continued leisurely towards the deck.

Sierra waited with bated breath as her parents walked up to the doors before flinging them open and waving them in.

"Hurry! The howls! A monster is out there!" she

rushed out in a panic.

Her mom and dad exchanged a look while closing the door behind them. Her dad dropped to one knee, motioning for her to come closer.

"Honey, that's just a coyote, or a wolf. They live out here, so we're going to hear howls a lot, okay? But you don't have to worry. As long as you're careful and don't go near them, they won't really bother you," he explained patiently.

Her mom nodded while flipping off the porch light. "Your daddy is right. Animals don't really like people. So, we just have to be careful while we're outside, but nobody is going to be eaten by a wolf or coyote while we're living here."

"But I saw—" Her daddy cut her off by ruffling her long hair.

"You might see them at the edge of the trees, but I promise we're all safe, okay? So, no more talk about monsters. It's only wild animals out there, and they deserve to live in these parts as much as we do," he stated.

Sierra pouted but nodded. "Okay."

"Good, now I think we were going to make some s'mores inside? Come on, my little chef, you can help me prep the crackers!"

Sierra offered her dad a small smile. "With extra chocolate?"

Felicia laughed. "Just this one time, I suppose. But then it's bath time, missy."

"Okay! Let's make s'mores!"

"That's my girl!" Rey cheered, scooping Sierra up and marching over to the kitchen. But even as they prepared to make a chocolate, gooey snack, Sierra couldn't keep her mind from the monster still hiding in her closet.

Her parents could promise that everything was okay when they didn't know that the monster was real. And he was hungry.

CHAPTER TEN

REY FROWNED as he stared at the deer outside the back doors. The herd had shrunk again, to about five grazing bucks and does. It seemed weird that within a week the numbers would drop so dramatically. Or maybe that was normal, but since he'd lived in the city his whole life, he didn't know it.

The weekend had finally arrived, and Felicia's mother had dropped by to pick up Sierra for some time away from the chaos of the house. She would only be gone a night, but already he missed his little princess. It was so quiet without her.

"So, what's the plan for today?" Felicia asked, turning the corner into the living room with an armful of laundry.

Rey shrugged. "I was thinking about going into town for that bird feeder you had mentioned. And maybe some bear spray or something. All of that howling makes me uncomfortable."

Felicia chuckled. "I thought there was nothing to worry about out here," she teased.

"There's not, but you can't be too safe or prepared," he muttered with a frown.

"Well, all right, want me to come with you?"

"Only if you want to."

Felicia shrugged. "I can do the laundry and some cleaning while you're gone. But I need you to pick up some more bleach, we're almost out."

Rey nodded and gave his wife a quick kiss on the cheek.

"Of course, baby. I'll be back soon."

"Don't rush on my account." She laughed.

Rey pulled the truck keys from his pocket and jogged out the back door to the garage. He grunted as he pulled the doors open, which still squeaked in protest. Still needed that lubricant that he was supposed to grab almost a week ago . . .

Rey added it to his mental list of supplies and slid into the driver's seat. He adjusted the mirrors, buckled up, then backed out into the driveway. The biggest challenge of the move so far was navigating their own driveway. He used the U-shaped curve around the front to turn the truck around and then crawled through the sharp turns and dips to the main road. Too many times his heart rate spiked as he thought that his brand new, sleek, black baby was about to hit a tree. The path was too narrow for his comfort. Maybe they needed to clear a few trees away and widen it. Or maybe he would get better at navigating the road the longer they lived here.

Nearly ten minutes later and he was finally headed into town. Though their house was hidden away in the trees and gave them the illusion of being completely secluded, they didn't live too far from major grocery stores and gas stations. In another fifteen minutes his truck was turning into town where people walked their dogs or pushed their kids in strollers down the streets, pausing to talk to one another in the beautiful warm afternoon.

It was what had first drawn him to moving away from the city. The loud noises of the buses shuttling down the street were gone. Parents didn't worry about their kids walking to school alone and being hit by a car going fifty-five down the road. Smaller towns held a unique kind of beauty to them that couldn't be recreated anywhere else. And the city, should they need it, wasn't that far away.

Rey pulled into the parking lot of a hardware shop and stepped out into the bright sun. This was what he wanted Sierra to see more of. Here she was more likely to make long-lasting friendships than back at their old apartment in Metro Detroit where the schools kept changing and bouncing the kids around every four years or so.

Locking the sedan, Rey started for the door with a smile on his face. The bell chimed as he walked inside the small store, packed with aisles of almost anything you could think of to repair or build a house. An older gentleman at the counter gave him a nod in greeting then turned back to the lady checking out. Rey nodded back and proceeded to browse through the expansive selection.

Marked down pepper spray, buy one get one free on WD-40, for a moment Rey wondered if he had hit the lottery. Nearly everything he needed was on sale. He never found deals this amazing back home—unless the wife did some couponing near the holidays.

"Need any help?"

Rey turned to look at the man from the register with peppered hair and a thick mustache. His eyes were kind as he peered down at the growing bundle of items in Rey's arms.

"Maybe a basket?" he offered.

Rey cleared his throat and nodded towards the back of the store.

"Actually, I think I'm just about finished. I'm just looking for something to keep any animals away from my house."

The older man nodded, in thought. "Got a raccoon problem?"

"No, we keep hearing these howls nearby and it's really spooking my daughter."

The man raised a brow and clarified, "Howls? Like dogs running loose?"

"I was thinking wolves or coyotes. Doesn't sound like a normal pup to me."

"I'm afraid to tell you that we don't have any wolves around here. And coyotes usually stay away because we're close to the city. Are you sure it's not a Labrador that got off the chain?"

Rey frowned. "I'm positive. Are you saying there is no way for it to be something else?"

"Well, no. I suppose a coyote could have wandered into the area, but he won't stay for long. Like I said, there's too many people around to make them comfortable," the man offered while leading him to the back.

"But we do have some traps you could set up to catch him if he gets too close. Or you can arm yourself with some tougher spray than that pepper spray in your hand. Just make sure to spray it downwind or it'll burn your face."

Rey nodded as he eyed the traps hanging from the wall.

"Most of these don't look like anything I could use in my backyard," he noted absently as he checked the price tags. Fifty dollars for a metal claw that could snag his daughter's ankle as easily as it could a rat. He didn't think so.

"Well, most of them are for hunting, not keeping a backyard free from critters," the man pointed out, pulling down a small black canister. "But this might do ya. Like I said, keep it away from your face, and downwind. Also, you could look into a gun if you're really concerned. Nothing will stop a bear with mange quicker than a bullet."

"We seriously have to worry about bears?" Rey asked.

The man cackled. "Of course, you live in Michigan and you're telling me that you've never heard of bears wandering around? Now, usually they keep to the upper peninsula, but we've found one or two in our area before."

"I lived down far enough that I never had to worry about any of this. I kind of thought my wife was being dramatic when she brought it up," Rey admitted as he grabbed a long hunting knife down from the shelf.

"Well, cougars are native here, too. Although you probably won't see one in your lifetime, outside of a zoo."

"That's a relief," Rey muttered, wondering briefly how his daughter would react to knowing large cats were roaming around outside as well. Maybe she would try to coax one inside as a pet . . . He shook the thought away and followed the man back up front to the register.

"Tell you what, if you find tracks of this creature in your backyard and bring the pictures to me, I'll help you pick some traps for it and give them to you half off," he offered.

"Really? Thanks, I appreciate that."

"Not a problem. Won't do anyone any good around here if something is sick and hanging around where the kids play. The sooner it's caught and moved, the better.

By the way, I'm Franklin, but everyone just calls me Frank."

Rey reached out and took Frank's hand in a hearty handshake with a smile.

"Pleasure to meet you, I'm Rey."

Frank rang up his order as he fished his wallet out of his pocket.

"Always nice to meet new folks around here. Was this everything for you?"

Rey froze. "Crap. I also need a bird feeder for my wife."

Frank laughed. "Not a problem, let me go get you one and you can head back home."

CHAPTER ELEVEN

FELICIA PULLED the last towel out of the dryer and shook it out before dropping the purple cloth into a basket. The washer tumbled and shook beside her, the timer claiming fifteen minutes left until the cycle was finished. With a sigh, she brushed off her hands and walked out of the laundry room behind the kitchen.

The house was blissfully quiet, interrupted only by a ding on her phone from the message Rey has sent her.

Want me to grab something for lunch?

She smiled and typed back *yes* before marching down the hall to the supply closet for the broom and dustpan. It felt good to do something normal after the chaos of packing and unpacking for their new home. Finally, everyone was settling in and finding new routines to their days. Rey would leave for work at five am, then Felicia would wake up at seven and get Sierra breakfast. Chores by nine, lunch at noon, and then playtime until dinner.

When school started in the fall everything would change again, but for now it was nice. It worked. It was beginning to feel like home.

Felicia closed the closet door and started back towards the living room when her daughter's room caught her eye. The door was cracked open and inside was an explosion of toys and blankets from an unkempt bed. She toed the door open further and stepped inside with a grimace. *Should have made Sierra clean up this mess before leaving*, she mused while bending down to pick up a stuffed bear.

Felicia tossed the toy back onto the bed and turned to pick up another when she spotted the pink blouse.

"God, Sierra, this was a perfectly clean shirt!" she moaned, scooping up the offending article and stomping over to the closet.

"I know I had this hanging up before she left . . ." she continued to mutter, sliding the door open to put the shirt away. Again. Her toe brushed something as she was leaning forward to grab an empty hanger, making her look down at the ugliest little figurine she had ever seen.

It was a wolf-like creature standing on its hindlegs with its claws poised like it was going to grab something. The muzzle was pulled back in a silent snarl with sharp, elongated teeth that barely fit in the opened mouth.

A shiver ran down Felicia's spine as she turned the figurine over in her hand. The fur stuck out like spikes, painted dark brown with a glossy protective coat. It was the monster Sierra had woken up screaming about just a few nights ago. But how did it get back inside of her bedroom? Did Sierra dig it out of the trash can? Why would she do something like that if the image of the creature terrified her so much?

Perhaps it was some sort of mistake, or misunderstanding . . . Felicia shook her head and clutched the figure tighter. That made absolutely no sense. It went into the trash can. The reappearance was deliberate. But why?

Felicia wandered out of her daughter's bedroom and into the living room where the sound of the doorknob turning brought her out of her churning thoughts. Rey pushed the door open with overstuffed grocery bags hanging from his left arm. He flashed her a quick smile before pushing his way into the house, kicking the door shut behind him, and tucking the truck keys into his right pocket.

"Need any help with those?" she offered as Rey lumbered his way to the kitchen island.

He shook his head. "Nah, I'm all right. But I left your bird feeder in the truck. I'll go back out and grab it in a bit."

The bags clanged when he heaved them onto the marbled countertop and slid them free from his arm. Curious, Felicia stepped over and peeked inside at an array of items, ranging from a discounted hammer to bear spray.

Cocking an eyebrow, she turned to her husband who was digging in the fridge for a water bottle and asked, "Do we really need all of this stuff? What is it for?"

He pushed the fridge door closed and twisted off the cap to the bottle. Taking a swig of water, he swallowed and shrugged.

"Well, the house needs some minor repairs that I can't do without some of that stuff, and I grabbed some extras so that I don't need to rush back out when something else falls apart."

"And the bear spray?" she inquired.

"Sierra's been worried about the howling at night. I figured the spray would make her feel better, and to be honest, it makes me feel a little better, too. The animals are too close around here. God only knows what's going to wander up on our porch one day. I'd rather be safe than sorry."

Felicia glanced down at the ugly creature clutched in her hand with a frown. Rey watched her and nodded at her curled fingers with a jerk of his chin before taking another drink.

"What's that?"

Felicia sighed heavily and placed the creature on the counter next to the plastic bags.

"The reason I want to shake our daughter. Look what she pulled out of the trash."

Rey choked on his water, nearly dropping the bottle as he reached out blindly for the counter edge behind him. His body bowed as the sputters turned into hard coughs. Felicia rushed around the island to his side, gently taking the bottle from his hand and setting it aside as she patted his back. After a few long minutes, the coughing finally died down into soft pants as Rey wiped his mouth with the back of his hand and slowly stood back up. Felicia grimaced, pulling a decorative towel off of a gleaming cabinet handle and passing it to her husband.

"Are you okay?"

Rey shook his head as he turned to the sink to wash his hands. "Felicia . . . I put that figure in the trash, then tied up the bag and took it to the barn."

She froze. "You did what?"

"I took the bag outside. I never left that thing in the house. Why would Sierra go out to grab it, and how did she know it was there? How would she have done it without us seeing her, or hearing her, go out?" His voice was low as he turned off the faucet and dried his hands on the proper towel.

Slowly he turned around to face his wife, his expression grave as he motioned back to the figurine.

"Unless she is *that* obsessed with the toy, I don't think she would have gone through all of the trouble to get it back."

Felicia shook her head. "That doesn't mean she didn't do it. For Christ's sake, Rey, how else did it get back inside? The damned thing isn't alive, it couldn't just walk through the door!"

He put his hands up in surrender. "Okay, fine, why

don't we just end this thing once and for all."

Rey paused for a moment as Felicia crossed her arms and eyed him warily.

"Why don't we just burn the stupid thing? Sierra won't be able to put it out of the trash if it's ash."

"Your serious?" she scoffed.

"Completely serious."

Felicia rolled her eyes, grabbing the seemingly harmless, ugly creature off the island. "That seems like a bit much. Why don't we just throw it out again? And replace whatever trash bag she ripped into to get it out while we're at it."

Rey shrugged and grabbed his water bottle again.

"All right, fine. We'll do that. I still want to have a bonfire tonight."

She chuckled. "Fine, we'll do the bonfire afterwards. We could even get fancy and roast something over the flames."

"Sounds like a plan to me."

Felicia beamed up at her husband. "Fantastic! Then could you grab the trash bag while you're over there?"

He gave her a crooked grin. "Sure, baby, anything for you."

She laughed and grabbed the figure off the counter. Her green eyes glittered as she danced around the island and strutted to the sliding glass door.

"Come on, Romeo!" she teased.

He chased after her with a laugh, following as she ducked out to the porch and ran down the short, wooden steps to the grass. As soon as her feet were flat again, he reached out and pinched her bottom, drawing a squeal out of her.

"Stop it!" she said, but her eyes belittled her words as she took off again, running across the grass to the old barn at the end of the driveway.

Rey followed a little over a foot away, watching as the most beautiful woman he knew giggled and danced around his outstretched fingers. For a moment it was easy to forget they were parents in their mid-forties, and not teenagers chasing one another in the fields behind the high school after class.

She finally lunged for the peeling black handle on the barn's side door and yanked the creaky thing open. It was one of the projects he would get to. Well, after today. The inside was dark and musty, with dust floating around that tickled their noses.

Felicia looked back at him with that gorgeous smile still gracing her lush lips as she stepped inside. He followed quickly, eager to finish cleaning up this crazy mess and get back to chasing one another around until, hopefully, they caught up with each other in bed again.

But what lay inside brought him to a halt and wiped the smile from his face. They stared at the trash can with blank expressions. The sounds of the wind gently ruffling the rafters almost masked their heavy breathing. Slowly they turned to one another and blinked. Rey held the trash bag, his fingers turning white as they dug further into the plastic. Felicia held the doll while fighting to find the words to describe what they had seen.

"I suppose we won't need the extra trash bag," she finally forced out.

He shook his head. "Nope. There is no mess to clean up in here."

That's exactly what made Felicia's blood run cold. The trash can looked undisturbed, with the bulging bag of garbage still neatly tied up in a bow and resting inside without so much as a teeny, tiny tear on the plastic. The can was nearly as tall as she was and was pressed against the warn wooden wall by the creaking side door.

She bit her bottom lip as she stepped around the can, her gaze sweeping over the dust covered floor. Nothing disturbed, no empty paint cans lying nearby or crates overturn for a step stool.

"So how did she do it?" Rey asked.

Felicia held up her hand as she walked back around the trash can, searching frantically for anything a five-year-old could use to climb up to the trash bag. Then carefully untie the bag, sort through the contains without dropping anything, and retie it . . .

She groaned, "Let's just burn the damn thing. I don't want to think about it. Our kid has to be some sort of magician, okay? Let's just . . . Let's just go."

Rey nodded slowly and motioned for her to walk out the door before him.

"All right, we'll burn it. And then?" he asked.

She scowled as she passed him and stepped out into the yard.

"Then we get a drink and call it a night," she called back.

He nodded again, turning with one last blank look at the trash bag.

"Yeah, that sounds like a good plan to me."

CHAPTER TWELVE

THE FIRE crackled as the long, bright flames reached for the heavens enshrouded in the dark midnight sky. Felicia watched it quietly with a glass of wine hanging loosely in her hand. The wolfman figurine curled and blackened in the middle of the pit. Her fingers itched to grab her phone and tape the event. It was an overwhelming urge to keep proof that this moment was real, which she fought hard to suppress. From the thin press of Rey's lips, she could guess he felt similarly.

What was it about this toy that was so disturbing? What was it about this toy that convinced them so deeply that burning it wasn't enough?

Felicia shook her head and took a deep pull of her wine. Perhaps she should have chosen a stronger drink. Sleep was long gone, leaving the couple unnerved and lost to their thoughts as the chilly air stirred lazily around them. They hadn't even changed, but hastily thrown on coats and boots over their pajamas to start the flames. Finally, her husband broke the silence.

"Are we completely sure Sierra didn't pull this thing out of the trash?"

Felicia closed her eyes and leaned back in the plastic chair across the pit from him.

"I suppose we can't rule it out. She could have snuck out to the garage after digging through all of the trash cans in the house—without either of us knowing—then climbed up to untie the bag and carefully removed the toy, to pick up anything she may have dropped and retie the bag just as you had so we wouldn't notice . . . To then take the figurine that was giving her nightmares back into her bedroom," she drawled.

He scowled and muttered something under his breath while fiddling with his beer bottle.

Doubt sat soured in their stomachs as they both turned their gazes to the vague remains of the figure. It was charred into a tiny black stump, almost resembling a warped rock. A twig snapped in the depths of the forest at the edge of the property.

Rey snatched up a flashlight at his side and clicked it on to illuminate a startled deer. They held each other's gazes for a moment, the couple not daring to breathe, until the deer finally ducked its head and ran off as quickly as its long legs could take it.

Felicia cracked a small smile, looking at her husband who shrugged and held his beer up in a salute. She silently raised her glass in return, and they took sips in silent unity.

As the blaze slowly sank to the ashes, with the moon high and half full, they rose from their chairs and quietly packed up for bed. Rey dumped a pail of water on the flames, then stomped out the lingering embers while Felicia surveyed the woods one last time. Bats, bugs, and owls gave the nightlife a chorus of quiet songs. It was almost serene enough to put the toy behind them and move on. Lightning didn't flash and the ground didn't quack.

There was nothing special about the creepy figure. It was just a carving easily destroyed. The game was over.

Rey held out his hand to his wife, and she took it with a growing sense of ease. Together they walked back to the porch and climbed the wooden steps to the back door before Rey paused to give her a quick kiss.

"Want to count this as a date night?" he asked with a crooked grin.

Felicia rolled her eyes with a chuckle.

"Oh yeah. Burning a doll that our daughter was obsessed with is definitely under the date night definition."

"Hey now, it helped set that sexy mood. Your wine and my beer. If that isn't romance, I don't know what is."

"Well, you're right. You don't know what romance is," she teased back with a quick peck to his cheek before sliding through the patio door.

Rey feigned offense as he chased his wife into the house, pausing to slide the lock of the door into place. He took in the sight of the beautiful woman before him, lit by the silver of the moon through the glass. She never failed to take his breath away.

Felicia bit her bottom lip while her eyes danced in anticipation as he stalked closer.

"Take that back," he growled with a wicked grin.

She waited with coiled muscles, springing away from his hand when they shot out to grab her.

"No," she giggled.

Rey licked his lips. "Remember our first date? The picnic at the Jefferson Field with a bouquet of daisies and my old guitar? Tell me that wasn't romantic."

"It wasn't. You sang like a dying walrus and played off-key the entire time. Then the flowers attracted bees and ruined the food," she said with a snort.

She shifted ever so slightly, cocking one hip to the side as she tossed her soft hair over her shoulder.

"Face it, Rey. Romance isn't your thing and if you want me to take it back—" She paused to lick her luscious lips. "You'll have to make me."

He lunged and, with a squeal, Felicia fled down the hallway, crashing through the bedroom door and narrowly escaped his grasp. He followed with an echoing laugh, kicking the door closed behind them.

CHAPTER THIRTEEN

"THANK YOU so much for taking Sierra for the weekend, Mom."

Felicia gave her mother a tight hug, drinking in the familiar scent of vanilla and fresh air. Her mother was an inch shorter than herself, and heavier, with a smile that reminded her of everything good in the world. Her mom's gray hair was pulled back into a bun, and as they parted, her gray eyes turned to follow Sierra as she ran to her bedroom.

She smoothed the skirts of her floral dress before addressing her daughter as a door closed soundly down the hall.

"So, how has everything been?" she asked carefully.

Felicia blew out a breath and waved her into the kitchen area.

"Want some tea?" she offered. Her mother nodded and waited, leaning against the kitchen island.

"Well, Sierra should be starting school soon. Rey is working pretty long hours, but it isn't too bad. I've had plenty of housework to keep me busy. We just finished unpacking everything," Felicia mused while filling the kettle with water.

Her mother nodded. "It isn't easy moving around. But how has your daughter been taking everything?"

Felicia paused, pursing her lips as she turned to face the older woman.

"What do you mean?"

"Well, . . . it's just that she was having nightmares at my house. I was wondering if you knew about that, if it was related to the move, or if maybe Sierra was hiding it from you all . . ."

Felicia sighed, running a hand through her hair as she tried to explain. "We knew. Sort of. I didn't know about the consistent nightmares exactly, but I'm not surprised. She found this doll in her bedroom and it was scaring her, so we got rid of it. I was hoping everything would stop once the damned thing was gone."

"She said that a dog-like creature was hunting her in the dreams. And that it killed you and Rey," her mother offered gently.

"Yeah, the doll was a dog—or maybe it was a wolf—like creature. I don't have a clue where it came from, but I'm positive that we will never see it again."

"Good, then hopefully everything will calm down soon."

Felicia pulled some tea bags and cups down from

the cupboard as the kettle began to squeal.

"I certainly hope so because the entire situation is driving me insane. I'm almost afraid that these nightmares and such will keep happening until after she's settled in school," she admitted, filling the glasses up and placing a bag in each one. She turned to her mother who took her cup with a grateful smile.

"It might. Stress aggravates fear and stirs a child's imagination. In fact, I remember our first big move when you were younger. You were convinced that there were ghosts in our vents and that one was going to come out and grab you," her mother mused. "Your father had to go with the bible and read a passage in every room of the house until you finally calmed down."

Felicia chuckled, blowing on her cup of tea before taking a small sip.

"How long did I freak out before Dad did that?"

"Oh, about a month—almost two. It was exhausting, but eventually it passed, just like I'm sure this one will."

Her mother turned to wander slowly into the living room, coming to a stop before the sliding glass door. Her eyes lit up as she gazed lovingly out into the backyard, prompting Felicia to grab her cup and follow.

Her mother nodded out at a group of three deer grazing by the tree line. Their long, graceful necks bent while their ears twitched and moved to the sounds of nature around them.

"That really is beautiful. I think I would sit in the living room every day if I got to watch the animals play around." Her mother sighed.

Felicia smiled, tilting her head as she watched a squirrel dart close to the deer in question. One of the does lifted their head to the newcomer, making the poor tiny squirrel pause and then quickly scamper off towards the driveway.

"Yeah, it really is beautiful out here," she mused.

"Well, I should be going. Rush hour on I-75 is horrendous, so I have to get moving if I want to avoid that."

Felicia turned as her mother finished her tea and walked back to the island to set the cup down.

"Are you sure? You could stay for dinner; I'm sure Rey would love to see you."

"Yes, unfortunately I promised Marge that I would help her with the bingo game tonight. But I promise to be back up soon to see you all," she replied reluctantly.

Felicia nodded and gave her mother another hug before yelling, "Sierra, come give Grandma a hug! She has to go home!"

A door swung open and the patter of tiny feet pounding down the hall followed. Sierra ran up to her grandmother with a bright smile, holding out her arms for a hug. The older woman chuckled as she bent down to scoop Sierra up into her arms. They embraced one another for a moment, the tender moment filling Felicia warmly. Her mother placed Sierra back on the ground and turned for the door, pulling her keys out of her pocket as she went. She gave a wave behind her as she pulled open the door and stepped out.

"Bye, honey, I love both of you!"

"Bye, love you, too!" Felicia and Sierra called back as the door slowly closed shut with a soft click.

They turned away, Sierra already animatedly relaying the events that happened at Nana's house. She got to eat cookies for breakfast one morning, Nana let her pick out a brand-new coloring book, and she got to help Nana paint a desk.

Felicia froze with a gasp, her feet almost in the hallway as Sierra skipped to the bedroom. Sierra paused and turned back to her mom.

"What's wrong?" she asked.

"Nothing, I just forgot to do something earlier," Felicia said with a quick smile.

"Do you want a snack?"

Her question was met with a squeal and dance of approval. She chuckled and walked through the kitchen to the fridge. Popping open the door, she browsed through the fruits and settled on a cluster of grapes.

Sierra watched as Felicia grabbed a bowl from the cupboard and began rinsing the grapes in the sink, pulling them from the stem and dropping each one into the plastic bowl.

"Sierra, honey, I'm going to turn on the television for you while you eat, but you have to stay at the coffee table with your food, okay? I need to go do something really quick. Can you be good while I get this thing done?"

Her daughter bobbed her head in agreement as she finished prepping the fruit. Snack in hand, Felicia led Sierra to the coffee table and set down the bowl. She turned on the TV, flipping through until she found some cartoons. With her baby all settled in, she set the remote back down on a side table and headed towards the stairs to the office.

"I'll be super quick, honey, but if you need me you can just yell and I'll come down, okay?"

"Okay!"

Felicia peeked back to make sure Sierra was still seated on the floor and absorbed into the screen. Satisfied, she nodded with a "good," and bound up the stairs.

In order to open the attic door, she had to drag the office chair over to the trapdoor and stand on the cushion in order to reach the latch keeping the door locked. The door swung down with her guiding hands and the ladder slid down into place with a few clicks. Pushing the chair back, she grabbed the ladder and carefully climbed up.

The floor had been swept up and the desk cleaned off. Most of the cobwebs from the corners of the room knocked down and cleaned up. A few boxes and totes were pushed off to the sides of the room, filled with miscellaneous items.

The desk stood in its glory at the back of the

room. The long, curved legs gleamed after a thorough polishing with a swirled design on the feet. Carefully carved patterns resembling leaves and columns continued all over the structure, accenting the top of the desk and the five drawers—two on each side, with one narrow, long drawer in the middle. The drawers had dark brass handles with knots in the middle of their design, and locks without a key. They all glided open and closed without an issue but were empty inside. It was beautiful and sturdy with only a few scratches on the top where the dollhouse had been discovered.

Felicia dug out her cellphone and quickly snapped a few photos of the front, top, and sides. The back was pressed against the wall, but she had enough images to get an idea of what she was working with. She sent the pictures off to a friend named Kimberly, who specialized with antiques. If this thing was worth anything, Kim should know. Task finally done—after how many weeks of planning to do it? Felicia turned to head back downstairs.

As she knelt on her knees to lower herself through the doorway, her phone dinged within her pocket. She pulled it back out and tapped on the text notification.

Does it have a secret drawer?

Felicia frowned, glancing back up at the desk and tapping back a *no* in reply. She cleaned most of the desk herself. She probably would have found it if there was one.

It looks Victorian era, but I would have to be there

in person to be sure. Thought it might have a secret compartment in it. Lots of them did.

Felicia climbed back onto her feet and approached the desk again.

Just curious, where would it be if it had one?

In one of the side drawers. Usually in the top or bottom. You gotta feel around for the latch.

Starting with the left top drawer, Felicia pulled open the door and started investigating again.

Might be in middle drawer now that I think about it.

Felicia rolled her eyes as she moved to the right bottom drawer and slid it open. So far everything felt like wood. And it was making her worry about getting a sliver as she searched for some sort of latch. The wood was rough, but as she pressed against it, she felt something give. A tiny little wiggle, but it was definitely loose.

Hope bloomed in her chest as she felt around the edges for a handle or something. It was all flat, but as she pressed around a soft click brought the ceiling down and a thick block of leather dropped on top of her wrist.

Felicia rocked back on her heels, using the glow of her phone screen to peer down at a small black book tied with red ribbon. She carefully pulled it out, examining the yellow pages and small knot in the material that clashed with the worn, aged journal. She quickly typed back to Kimberly in excitement.

Found it! Has a book in it! You're a genius!

That'll probably tell you how old the desk is, hun. Lemme know what it says.

Then she tucked the device away. The knot was pretty tight, and she feared that it would have to be cut away. As she pondered over what to do, she heard her daughter's voice faintly through the door. The interesting treasure would have to wait. Her baby needed her again.

Felicia sighed and placed the book back in the drawer, closing it so nothing could get to it before she was ready. Then she stood up and walked to the trapdoor. With one last longing look at the desk, she lowered herself down to the ladder and closed the attic up behind her.

CHAPTER FOURTEEN

THE CLOUDS churned angrily, casting the world below in long shadows broken only by the streaks of light that sliced down from the heavens. It was a war outside that crashed together with a deafening roar. Wind pelted the sides of the house, causing the wood to creak and groan against the assault. The windows shuddered as the rain slammed against the glass, driving down in buckets that drenched everything it touched in mere seconds. Another *crack*! And light flashed inside of Sierra's room, lighting up her dollhouse and the toys left scattered on the floor.

She sat on the floor at the end of her bed, tucked into a tight ball with her hands clamped tightly against her ears. She squeaked when the rumble of the storm filled the space again, giving her only a brief moment to brace herself against another streak of lightning. She clenched her teeth, trying to block out the noise rumbling around her.

It was just a storm. It wasn't a monster, or anything bad that she needed to be afraid of. Mommy told her this every time one came through. Yet that did little to soothe her nerves.

Amidst the tempest a strange sound touched her ears. It was easy to miss but sent a new wave of icy dread through her body when she focused on it. The scuffle of wood sliding against wood slowly moved in between the crashes of thunder. She froze as the fear of the new noise dominated her mind until it became more pressing than the storm itself. What was it? Where was it coming from?

Images of a large hairy beast with spindly fingers and razor-sharp teeth popped into her mind. It reached out with a low growl, scraping its nails against the floorboards as it pulled itself out from under her bed. With a shriek, Sierra threw herself forward, crawling across the floor until she reached the safety of her door. Her heart pounded as she turned to face her familiar wooden bedframe. Her comforter was draped over the edge, hiding most of what lay underneath. That strange sound came again.

With shaking limbs, Sierra pulled herself back over to her original hiding place. The room was dark as she lowered her face to the floor and reached up to grab her blanket. She swallowed against the fear that threatened to overwhelm her and repeated her mommy's words to herself again.

"It's just a storm. It's not a monster. It's just a storm. It's not a monster."

Crack!

Sierra yanked the blanket out of the way as light filled her bedroom, illuminating the space underneath. It was empty. Relief stole her strength, and she collapsed onto the floor with her eyes stinging with tears. No monsters. Just a storm. Mommy was right again. The sky seemingly rumbled in agreement.

A few minutes passed before she finally slowed her rapidly beating heart and stopped shaking uncontrollably. Funny that the immediate threat of the monster had passed and yet, she still wasn't as afraid of the storm as she had been only ten minutes before. The loud noises didn't seem as deafening now. The rain wasn't as violent pelting the window. Even the wind that tried to shake the house seemed lighter and easier to listen to.

Then it came again, and her heart skipped a beat. Wood slid against wood softly, however, the sound didn't stop. It continued to make its path somewhere within her bedroom. The trailing sound sent shivers down her spine.

Sierra pulled herself up onto her hands and knees, darting quick glances around the floor. Where was the noise coming from? What did it mean?

"It's just a storm. It's not a monster," she huffed to herself.

The lightning flashed in the room, throwing long

shadows on the walls. One shadow was gliding past a very tiny window in a very tiny house. The light left, plunging everything into darkness again as Seirra continued to stare at her wall. She held her breath, her mind spinning over what she saw. The flash came and sure enough the shadow was moving still.

Gathering her courage, Sierra crawled over to her dollhouse with her breath coming out in short, quick pants. She peered down inside at her family of dolls and watched as the mama replica slid down the hallway. The wooden base of the doll's "feet" scratched against the wooden surface of the floor.

Sierra didn't know what to do. Scream? Cry? Hide? She didn't understand what was going on or how it was happening. As the doll finally came to a stop outside of the new bedroom, she heard the rattle of her own doorknob turning. The replica of herself slowly turned around as Sierra moved to face whatever was coming inside.

The door swung open, and Felicia blinked down at her daughter, who looked pale with her small mouth gaping open.

"Sierra, honey, what are you doing?"

Sierra started to cry, holding her arms out for her mother to scoop her up. Soothing murmurs were whispered in her ear as the thunder clapped through the sky.

"It's okay, baby. It's just a storm. It's nothing to be afraid of," Felicia promised as she walked over to the side of the bed. Her daughter shook her head, burying her mouth in her mom's purple pajama top with her eyes peeking just over her shoulder.

Her mom was wrong. Because her mom didn't see the figurine standing at the front door of the tiny dollhouse, lit up as the streaks of lightning crashed from outside. The monster was back, and it was ready to eat them.

CHAPTER FIFTEEN

REY MUTTERED a string of curses as he lugged a thick tree branch, nearly as long as himself, from the middle of the driveway. The storm had torn through the area, ripping branches from the trees and even setting fire to someone's shed a few streets down. Thankfully, they didn't seem to have any damage to their property so far. The garage had somehow withstood the high winds and while he didn't fully investigate the building, it appeared completely unharmed. The house was fine, and his truck—which was stupidly left outside—was still standing without any scratches or dents.

It could have been so much worse. That didn't make the cleanup any more enjoyable to do as his shoes sunk down into the mud that used to be the backyard. With a grunt, Rey heaved the branch off into a growing pile of rubbish near the foot of the deck. He brushed his hands off on his dirt-caked jeans and toyed with the idea of heading inside for a glass of iced tea. Then he dismissed it since he had only put in maybe twenty minutes of actual work on their yard.

It was late in the afternoon, with the sun shining brightly overhead and warm winds ruffling his hair. The rest of the forecast for the week was sunny with high temperatures, which he hoped would soak up the excess rain quickly. A small pond had been created overnight, near the far edge of the property. He was worried that as soon as Sierra saw it, she would want to swim in it. They were going to have to keep her pretty busy inside until it shrunk enough not to be tempting.

His shoes sunk into the soft earth as he made his way around the back of the garage. His gaze flitted across the ground to watch for holes or sticks in the way. Another large branch was resting near the whitewashed paneling of the back wall, missing the structure by mere inches. Again, he sent up a silent prayer of gratitude for their luck in avoiding any serious damage. He bent down at the thick base where the wood snapped from the tree and grabbed ahold of it with both hands. Standing back up, Rey started the slow journey back towards the deck.

Dragging the offending object was destroying what little grass they still had. Rey had high hopes it would grow back within a few weeks. Of course, he never learned much about lawn care before moving out to a massive yard to care for. Maybe it needed some mulch or something. He made a mental note to look it up online when he was done.

Felicia stared out the sliding door as he added the dead weight onto the pile. He huffed and wiped his hands off on his jeans again as she popped her head outside.

"Need any help?" she offered.

Rey shrugged then shook his head. "Not unless you want to be a sweetheart and grab me a glass of tea. Maybe you could set it on the railing, and I'll grab it when I came back with more crap from our yard."

She rolled her eyes but flashed him a smile. "I think I can manage that. Want any lemon in it?"

"No thank you, just lots of ice. It's getting surprisingly warm out here for the middle of August."

"No problem," she called out before closing the door and wandering deeper into the house.

Rey took another breath before releasing it with a grumble. He marched towards the back of the garage again to check the forest line for anything that could be a hazard to Sierra when they finally let her outside. For a moment he toyed with the idea of calling off work the next day. Maybe he could pretend to have a cold and finish everything up in the morning. But he dismissed it. It wouldn't be fun, but he could get the place back into decent shape in a day. Less if he stopped bitching to himself and worked.

The property stretched out past the thick of the trees for another forty feet. They rarely went traipsing back so far, but technically they owned it all, and the previous owners had a dirt pathway carved into the land for riding bikes or walking. They also owned another chunk of the yawning grass next to the driveway that was more or less ignored since it sloped down to another line of trees that hid god only knows what in the branches. Bees' nests, rabid raccoons, possibly bear . . .

Rey was too busy looking up at the looming branches overhead that he missed his step and slid down the slope that he warned his family away from. He let out a yelp as his shoes slid in the mud and went out from under him. He tumbled the short distance down into the waterlogged ditch, coughing as the dirty water splashed up in his nose. His body ached as he quickly pushed himself up and spat out as much of the grime and sludge as he could. His stomach turned to think of what might be swimming, or dead, in the swallow storm reminiscence.

"Goddamn it!"

Rey stood up, swearing loudly as he wrung out the front of his soaked shirt and glared angrily at his cold, wet jeans. Mud clung to his hair, dripping down the sides of his face and streaking against his skin as he wiped it away. He looked around the dense forest around him and groaned when he spotted a dead deer carcass almost eight feet away towards the back of the property.

That made his day perfect.

"Leave it and attract scavengers, or drag it up the

hill to the garage?"

Neither of the ideas sounds particularly pleasant, but he didn't want to deal with any surprises later on, either. Rey watched his footing as he approached the dead animal, pausing with a dry heave when he saw the extent of damage done to the poor thing. It looked ravaged, the stomach completely torn out and the throat half shredded. One of the legs was missing, and the head was bent back enough to almost touch his forehead to his bloodied back. Flies swarmed around the open flesh, buzzing loudly. The smell was worse than anything he had endured before.

His stomach churned but what rooted his feet before the gruesome sight was the disturbed piles of mud around the deer. And the one massive paw print that was pressed into the watery ground. It was unlike anything he had ever seen before. The heel was long and wide, shaped like a warped heart from the foot pad of a bear or dog, with long extending toes. The claws had dug deep into the earth, and stretched out like talons, curling into the dirt by maybe two inches.

Once the shock wore off, Rey fumbled in his pocket for his cellphone and quickly took a few photos of the footprint. Then he walked around the deer and took a few photos of that carnage as well. The man at the hardware store had asked for tracks or something to help identify the creatures in the woods. Perhaps he would be able to explain the strange markings. Because as it stood, Rey didn't have any answers for what he saw.

If he believed in Heaven or Hell, he might be tempted to think that Hell had opened its gates in his backyard. Because whatever made those tracks and tore into that deer certainly wasn't going to be friendly. And it would definitely be back.

Rey pocketed his phone and spun away from the sight. Moving as quickly as the ground would allow him, he raced back up the slope and cut through the backyard to the porch. His glass of iced tea was waiting on the railing, almost getting knocked over as he rushed up the steps and to the back door. He slid the glass door open harder than he had meant, making the panel shake and quiver as it collided suddenly with the end of the track.

Not pausing to fix it, he kicked off his shoes and went stomping through the living room to the hall. Felicia stepped out of their bedroom, her eyes growing wide when she took in his disheveled state.

"What happened?" she asked as he pushed past her to the bathroom adjoined to their suit.

"I fell in the mud. Look, I don't mean to run past you, but I need to shower and then go into town for some supplies."

She gave his back a quizzical look as he yanked open one of the dressers to pull out clean jeans and a shirt.

"Supplies for what?"

He paused, a dark look shadowing his face before he masked it underneath cool indifference and lied.

"Nothing much. Just something to help me clean everything up before tomorrow. Don't worry about it, I've got everything under control."

CHAPTER SIXTEEN

THE TRUCK bumped along the road as Rey pulled off the dirt road and into town. His knuckles were stark white on the black steering wheel as he adjusted his speed, gritting his teeth against having to slow down. He needed to get to the store quickly; it was already 4:46 pm and would close soon. And more than that, he desperately wanted answers. He wanted someone to laugh and call him a city boy then explain what sort of hellish beast left those marks that the locals were used to dealing with. He kept comparing it to a man and bear, or dog hybrid. Despite it being completely impossible, the long and distinct toes on the print gave him the impression of a human's anatomy. Everything else screamed animal. A large, deadly animal that had crossed his property line during the night and killed without anyone aware it was even there.

Hell, it probably ventured past the firepit to that

pond of water for a hearty drink after its meal. Again, the urge to vomit rose. Rey didn't think of himself as thin-skinned, but some things were too disgusting to ever forget. And that image of the deer would stay fresh in his mind for the next few months. He had never seen anything like it. He hoped again that Frank would be able to tell him it was completely normal. Just a coyote. Or something. Didn't he mention cougars? Could that be it?

Rey shook his head, trying to clear the jumble of thoughts away when the small brown building finally came into view. It was next to a convenience store, just past the red light. Letting out a breath he hadn't realized he had been holding, Rey settled back in his seat and uncurled his fingers from the wheel. He gave them a flex, wincing when tiny needles of pain shocked through them.

The light turned green, and he eased the truck into the parking lot, feeling a rush of relief when he realized his vehicle was the only one in the lot. It would be easier to explain the entire situation without anyone else getting involved. Well, he silently amended, he didn't want anyone getting involved yet. If it turned out that this thing was a real threat, then he would follow the proper channels to get the proper help out to his yard. Maybe a team to help lift that carcass away from his family's home, at the very least.

Rey turned off the ignition and pulled out his keys, jamming them in his pocket as he yanked open the truck door. The vehicle swayed as he jumped out and slammed the door shut, remembering only halfway to the front door to press the lock on the fob. The bell rang above him as he stepped into the store, startling poor Frank who was fiddling with a box of bolts at the counter.

"Hey there Rey, how are you doing?" Frank greeted him with a smile, putting the box under the counter. "Anything I can get for ya? A new bird feeder?"

Rey paused, blinking twice before remembering that he never put the darn thing up.

"Uh, no, it survived the storm," he muttered. It would probably survive the next one too if he forgot it again. "I came to talk to you about that animal that was walking around my property."

"Oh, yeah? Finally catch it?" Frank asked, leaning over the counter as Rey dug out his cellphone.

"No, but I have some pictures to show you. I found its tracks, and I was hoping you could tell me what it might be."

The older man nodded in understanding, tilting his head as he was presented with one of the images. He stared at it for a moment, his lips pressing into a thin line as Rey swiped over to the next photo of a closeup of the claw marks.

"I also found a deer nearby these marks. I have pictures of that, too, if you want to see. It's gruesome, though," he warned.

Franklin cleared his throat, his thick gray brows

pinching together.

"Let me see them."

Rey nodded, swiping the screen again to pull up the next image. The man didn't flinch from the sight, but his expression became more concerned with each second that passed by. Finally, he pulled away and nodded towards the device.

"You didn't stage those, boy? Are you sure those are real?" His tone bordered on angry, drawing out an agitated response from Rey.

"And why the hell would I fake this shit? I don't want some sort of massive creature in my yard—and I sure as hell don't want a dead deer lying in it either!"

Frank narrowed his eyes for a moment before he stepped around the front counter and ambled to the front door. Rey watched him warily, putting his phone back in his pocket. Frank flipped the open sign around and shook his head, muttering something under his breath as he did it.

"Do you know what this is or not?" Rey demanded, crossing his arms over his broad chest.

Frank sighed, turning around to face him with an expression that looked aged beyond his years. His wrinkles stood out around the corners of his mouth and around his eyes. For a moment Rey felt guilty about barking at the man. It wasn't his fault that he was so tightly wound up, but he was becoming desperate for something. And being silent wasn't helping soothe his nerves at all.

Finally, Franklin spoke, "I have seen that before. Only once, mind you, and it was a long time ago. I wasn't sure I believed it then, and I'm not sure I believe it now."

"What is it?" Rey pressed.

"I can show you a picture. I think that'll help more than words. Can you drive over to my place?" Frank raised a hand when Rey opened his mouth to protest. "Trust me, now. Some things are better seen than heard about."

Rey gritted his teeth but nodded.

"All right, tell me where I'm going."

CHAPTER SEVENTEEN

IT **WAS** getting darker, and Rey still wasn't home.

Felicia stared out at the pile of branches through the sliding doors with a cup of tea in her hands. Sierra sung along to her program behind her, the image on the television reflecting faintly on the glass. Purple gumdrops danced with bright yellow blobs while a smiling sun played the guitar over top of the mess outside. Honestly, it didn't look too bad, all things considered. She could probably grab a garbage bag and start putting the smaller branches and twigs inside of it for trash day. They couldn't clean when the sun went down, so she might as well do something while they still had an hour or two left in the day.

If nothing else, she would be able to get most of the pile packed away. Then Rey wouldn't have to worry about it before heading off for work.

"Sierra, are you going to be okay if I go outside and

clean up the yard?" she mused.

"I thought Daddy was cleaning up the yard?"

Felicia turned away from the window and walked to the kitchen sink, setting her cup down on the island as she passed it by.

"Yes, but Mommy is going to go out and help him while he is in town grabbing more supplies."

"Oh. Okay! I'll be fine," Sierra called back, flopping down onto the couch as the song finally ended and the gumdrops moved on to tell a story about a mouse.

Felicia pulled open the cabinet under the sink and reached down into the black box of garbage bags. She came up empty.

"Damn," she muttered under her breath. Guess that was what Rey was in a hurry to run and buy. Well, there went her plans to try and help. She could put on some boots and try to drag some of the thick branches from the back tree line to the deck, but she had the strength of a hamster and wouldn't make it too far.

Not that she would ever admit that to Rey.

She closed the door and leaned against the sink with a frown. Maybe they had spares in the hall closet. When they moved in, she tucked some cleaning supplies away in there because she didn't have enough room under the sink. She might have put a second box up on the top shelf. Or maybe it was a box of cleaner? Pushing away, she wandered down the hall to check.

The closet was at the end of the hall with a thin wooden door and fake gold doorknob. It squeaked when she pulled it open, making her cringe slightly and added fixing that issue onto the list. She should text Rey once she was done to pick up WD-40 while he was out.

The bottom three shelves held extra linens and blankets while the top two had extra toiletries and the cleaners she couldn't store elsewhere. She pushed aside the bottles of polish and air freshener with her fingertips, standing as high as she could on her tiptoes to peer in the back. She saw the top of a black box but couldn't read the description from her level and cursed quietly again. Being short sucked sometimes.

Finally admitting defeat, she rocked back to the flats of her feet and stepped away.

"Where did I put the step stool?" she muttered to herself while wondering if it was even worth grabbing. She could just wait for Rey to get back . . .

A small clatter made her pause next to Sierra's bedroom door. She frowned, peeking around the corner to double-check that her daughter was still dancing in the living room to the gumdrops before reinvestigating the sound.

She opened the door and stepped inside, mindful of the toys scattered across the floor. It was a minefield of miniature blocks, dolls, and doll accessories with a random sock or two thrown into the mix.

"I thought I told her to clean this mess up before she could watch TV," she grumbled, pushing a tiny purple shoe out of her path. It was her fault for not double-checking before turning the screen on. Sierra was usually a very good girl, but she hated cleaning up her room.

Felicia knelt on the floor and started gathering up the closest toys. She tossed a stuffed giraffe onto the unmade bed. Flung the sock towards the door to grab on her way out. Then scooped up one of the beds from the dollhouse that lay overturned on the rug.

She leaned towards the house and carefully set it back inside the parents' room while noting that the daddy doll was missing. Even curiouser was the little Sierra doll that stood in the living room, facing the miniature fireplace and the doll of herself stood in the middle of the bright pink bedroom, facing a little cardboard dollhouse.

"Well, that's weird," she muttered leaning back.

A soft scratching noise drew her away from the dolls. It was close. And still moving. The hairs on the back of her neck stood up as she leaned around the dollhouse towards the sound. Her heart stopped and ice filled her veins. She opened and closed her mouth, but no sound would come out. What could she even say?

The dog-like doll was back and in perfect condition. The sharp spikes of its hair unmarred from the flames that she knew devoured it days ago. The tiny beady red eyes stared at her with the claw-tipped hands outstretched to grab its victim.

And. It. Was. Moving.

The base of the figurine scraped along the

floorboards as it glided towards the side of the replica house. It looked like it was being pulled by an invisible force. And while she stared at the damned thing, it never stopped. It moved closer and closer to where the built-in garage would have been.

Slowly she sat back, her breath coming out quickly as her wide eyes finally yanked themselves away from the creature. She silently stared inside the dollhouse as her hands started to shake, wishing she could scream. Yell. Do something!

Then the mommy doll from the pink room turned and faced her. And she got her wish.

Felicia tipped her head back and released a bloodcurdling scream.

CHAPTER EIGHTEEN

FRANK LIVED about five miles from the shop, down a long dirt road that held maybe four other houses and an old church that had seen better days. His house wasn't as far back from the street as Rey's was. Its whitewashed siding could be seen from the road with old, green painted flower beds underneath green shuttered windows. The boxes were empty and needed some touchups as the paint was cracked and some of the wood looked splintered. The porch was covered with a screened-in sitting room where a worn folding chair lay open next to a tiny metal table with an ashtray in the center of it.

Frank led Rey through the front door into a small living room with a rabbit-eared television and an overstuffed gray couch. A small coffee table was littered with takeout containers and empty soda cans. They walked over the orange carpeting into the attached kitchen area with moss green floor tiles and cream-colored walls. Frank stopped at one of the drawers and yanked it open, digging through the miscellaneous contents inside. He muttered to himself, a habit that Rey suspected the old man did when he was stressed out, before slamming the drawer closed and yanking open another one.

The kitchen table was small with dark green vinyl covering over it and two mismatched chairs pushed in. He toyed with the idea of sitting down when the drawer was slammed shut and Frank huffed in annoyance.

"Go ahead and get settled. I think it's upstairs with the other clippings. I'll be right back. Help yourself to a soda or beer in the fridge."

Frank nodded and then rushed off before Rey could get a word in, leaving him alone to wander around. The refrigerator was relatively new; the gleaming metal surface at odds with the older, worn appliances. A dish towel was hung at the bottom of the door handles, decorated in daffodils and lace.

Rey raised a brow as he inspected the inside shelves. Mostly cans of drinks rested on the clear, plastic surfaces. With a block of cheese covered in plastic wrap, a small tub of butter, some lunch meat, and a loaf of wheat bread. Snagging a can of cola, Rey shut the fridge door and sat down at the kitchen table in a hard, wooden chair with spokes missing from the back frame. As soon as he took a sip of his drink, Franklin stormed into the room with a wrinkled newspaper in his hands.

"Found it. Here, this should give you some answers on those footprints."

Carefully, Rey took the paper from Frank and eyed the front story dubiously. According to the date on the top of the page, the story was published almost thirty years ago. The title would have made him scoff, but the faded image below it stopped him.

"Dogman of Michigan—is it a Hoax?"

The picture was of a footprint, with a long, wide heart-shaped pad and four long toes that extended out with curved claws that had been sunk deep within the earth. It was damn near the exact same picture that he took.

"What is this?" he growled, scanning the article, which spoke about a man who claimed to see a massive dog-like creature wandering in front of his house at night. He finally caught a picture of a footprint left behind, but obviously nobody seemed to believe him.

"Have you ever heard of the Dogman?" Frank asked, settling into the chair across from him.

"I read about it online a long time ago," Rey muttered.

The dog creature was known as the urban legend of the state—*the Dogman*. A beast that stood on two legs like a human but retained the body of a canine. It was supposed to be clever, quick, and deadly. The beast roamed Michigan but tended to stay in the more wooded parts like Bigfoot. It was never seen, never photographed, but a few people found some tracks in the dirt and claimed it came from it.

"It's a story to scare people during camp. You don't honestly believe this thing is real? I mean, how does that make sense?"

Frank shrugged. "A lot of people around here do. You ever meet Laura? A lil nutty but sweet as pie and believes whole heartedly that the Dogman wanders our forests. Her house has a big sign in the front yard if you wanna go ask her about it—and I think ya should."

He pointed at the picture on the front of the paper. "Personally, I've never seen it but tell me how it makes sense that you have that same image on your phone right now. So, unless you faked that muddy print, I would say that the Dogman is as real as anything else is. Unless, of course, you have any better ideas?"

Rey ground his teeth, tossing the paper onto the table, and snatching up his soda for a quick swig. Of course, he didn't have any ideas. He came from the city. He'd never seen a possum until three weeks ago. Hell, he hadn't seen deer outside of zoos, either. Unless they were dead on the side of the road, but that didn't count. Maybe it was just something more obscure?

Frank chuckled darkly, reading the thoughts pass through Rey's eyes.

"You could take your picture to the library and compare it to the wildlife around here. Or go straight to animal control with it, they will take a good look at that for ya. You could even go to the sheriff, but

I'm tellin' you we're all going to say the same thing. Maybe you're right and it isn't the Dogman, but do you have any other name for something that leaves behind markings like that?" he asked, leaning on the kitchen table.

Rey shook his head slowly.

"Exactly. Now this thing has been here once before, and last time things didn't end so pretty. So, it's my best advice to you to stop thinking about whether or not a legend is possible and start worrying about whether or not you can stop it."

"What happened last time this thing came around?" Rey asked thickly.

Frank grabbed the newspaper and flipped to the middle where the rest of the story hid. He scanned the article for a moment before nodding and setting it down, the printed letters facing right side up for Rey. His bony finger tapped the third paragraph, chilling Rey as he read the passage out loud.

"Aaron Fuller was found dead inside his house Tuesday morning by the Fayeville sheriff after reports of hearing screaming in the area. He was presumed mauled to death by a wild animal."

No image accompanied the breakthrough, but there didn't need to be one for Rey to envision what had happened. He swallowed thickly, shaking the image from his mind.

"But nobody saw it since then, right? So, it might just be migrating or something?"

Frank looked at him for a moment before nodding thoughtfully.

"That's true, it might just be passing through and it's nothing to worry about. But I don't think I would bet my life on that."

Rey scrubbed a hand down his face, trying to wrap his mind around the impossibility of this situation. It was hard to accept, yet he couldn't deny what he had seen—both in the picture in the newspaper and with his own eyes. No known animal made those tracks.

"Okay, so what do I use to catch it?"

Frank shrugged. "I recommend a gun."

CHAPTER NINETEEN

"A GUN, you can't be serious." Rey blanched.

Frank levelled a steady gaze at the man in front of him.

"It mauled a man to death inside his own home. If I had a family like you, I would pick up anything I could to make sure that beast never took another breath again. Yeah, I'm serious. Get. A. Gun."

Rey scrubbed a hand down his face, his breathing uneven as he wrestled with the idea. He loved his family more than life itself. He couldn't see anything happen to them. Ever. It wasn't the thought of owning a gun that bothered him. But legally there were steps to go through for these sorts of things. And getting a gun without having those legal means was impossible.

Frank's eyes softened when Rey voiced his concerns, and he nodded in understanding before sliding his chair back. He took a deep breath then heaved himself onto his feet. He shuffled across the small kitchen area to a drawer next to an outdated stove covered in dust. From that drawer he pulled out a piece of black metal with the barrel aimed at the ground.

Rey's eyes widened as he watched the man approach the table again and set the piece of machinery on the table with the end pointed safely away from either of them.

"You can have mine for now. I sure ain't using it for nothing. It has a bit of a kick to it but nothing you can't handle. Just aim and shoot when you see the damn thing. Don't hesitate no matter what. Remember, it's kill or be killed. Then I might put another bullet in it to be safe."

Rey licked his lips, staring at the gun resting on the tabletop. "Are you sure about this? It could come after you, too. Nothing is stopping the Dogman from coming after this whole town if it wanted to."

"True, but those prints were close to your house, not mine. I don't want you all to be unarmed during the night when it decides to come back out. Maybe nothing will happen, but in case it does." Frank paused to pick up the gun and thrusted it into Rey's hands.

"You're prepared."

Funny, because he certainly didn't feel that way.

His nerves were just as tightly woven as when he had left the house an hour and a half earlier to figure out what the pictures on his phone meant. His knuckles were stark white, clenched tightly on the steering wheel as he drove down the long road towards the house while the sun slowly set in the horizon. The gun that Frank gave him rested in the glove box of the car, causing most of the stress that plagued him. It was stupid to take it. It would have been even dumber not to.

The Dogman couldn't be real. To entertain such a thought was stupid. But the prints matched up perfectly. No other creature had feet like it.

His grip on the steering wheel tightened as he went around in circles. It existed. It didn't. It existed. It didn't. It existed and they were being hunted.

"Fuck! How am I supposed to tell Felicia about this!" he roared into the expanse of his truck.

Hey, honey, so we have a creature in the backyard that is killing animals and I'm afraid it's going to come after us. What is it? Oh, have you ever heard of the urban legend about the Dogman? Basically, it's a werewolf that doesn't transform back into a human. Its bite doesn't make humans into Dogmen either. It just looks like a dog that walks on two legs with really long limbs and it can kill you faster than you can scream. I saw a post about it online when I was getting ready for work awhile back. I think your cousin shared the article? Anyway, yeah, I don't have any proof except for these pictures of paw prints in the mud.

Oh, and nobody has ever caught solid proof of this creature. Somehow it avoids motion sensing cameras and is too quick for a camera phone to get. Nobody knows why. But yeah, it's definitely going to kill us. It's okay, though, because I got a gun from a man I've only spoken to twice now. I love you.

That was going to go perfectly. What could she possibly have to be worried about? She wouldn't question anything either, because it was just so obvious that she couldn't. He could even find very vague references about it online with super grainy photos as evidence.

"I'm fucked. We're all fucked," he muttered to himself as he pulled into the long driveway. The truck bounced as he hit an arching root too hard. His teeth were likely to shatter with how tightly he clenched them. Rey followed the narrow twisting path until the trees gave away and the house came into view.

Along with the monstrous creature standing a few feet from the garage door. Its body was covered in thick fur that stood out in short spikes along its long and slightly curved spine. The arms and legs were long and humanoid, but the clawed hands and feet with elongated toes and spindly fingers were anything but. A muzzle stretched out from the face of the beast, the lips pulled back to reveal two rows of sharp teeth and a line of spittle dripping from its chin. It was half man, half dog. All horror.

The bright amber eyes of the beast narrowed on his truck, and without a second thought, Rey slammed on the gas.

The truck lurched forward, the tires squealing and kicking up a spray of dirt as he held the wheel steady for his target. The Dogman opened its mouth and let out a piercing scream that sent chills down his spine before turning on its heel and running for the yard.

"Not so fast, fucker!" Rey screamed as he followed it through the yard. The truck inched closer, gaining on the creature as the engine roared its own battle cry.

The Dogman dropped down onto all fours and with one last look into Rey's eyes, he burst forward with unmatched speed to the safety of the thick line of trees.

Rey gasped as he slammed on the brakes, yanking the wheel as the vehicle struggled to stop on time. The side of the truck tipped slightly as it slid sideways before locking into place and falling back down all four tires in the soaked earth, spraying mud up in the process. Rey yanked off his seatbelt and flipped open the glove box. The gun slid into his open palm as he threw the door open and jumped into the torn grass. He flipped off the safety as he rounded the front of the truck and aimed into the trees.

He could barely make out the tail of the Dogman as it raced away from their property. He squeezed off a round, but the bullet missed with a spray of bark as the creature dodged left and slipped out of view.

His hands started shaking as he slowly lowered the gun. He wasn't crazy. It really did exist. And it had almost gotten to his family.

Rey flipped on the safety with shaking hands as

he walked back around the truck towards the house. His daughter and wife stood at the glass doors, both watching him with horror and confusion etched into their faces. The relief of seeing them alive and unharmed almost brought him to his knees.

Felicia looked down at their daughter and said something. Sierra nodded and darted off. His wife yanked open the sliding glass door and stared at him for a moment longer, her mouth opening and closing again, wordlessly.

Rey climbed the stairs of the deck as the tears started to slip down her face.

"Rey," she finally croaked. "What's going on?"

He took a deep breath and set the gun on the patio table before pulling her into his arms.

She was stiff at first, croaking out another confused, "Rey?"

"It's going to be okay, baby. I promise. I know we need to talk, but I really need this right now," he murmured, pressing his nose into her hair. She nodded, digging her fingers into his back as she pulled him tighter against her. He started shaking harder, burying his face into the crook on her neck as she kept him close. Her fingers smoothed out, rubbing his back as they started gently rocking together.

"It's okay. It's going to be okay," his voice cracked as he repeated it softly to her.

Felicia swallowed thickly, pressing a kiss to the side of his head as her shoulder grew damp.

"I know, Rey. It's going to be okay."

CHAPTER TWENTY

"SHOULD WE leave?" Felicia asked quietly.

"Where are we going to go?" Rey asked back.

It had been an hour since the incident. The night blanketed the sky with an eerie silence that kept the family on edge. Sierra was tucked away in their bedroom, watching a movie to help ease her mind from the attack. Rey had called off work claiming to have food poisoning while Felicia tucked their daughter in.

Now they sat quietly at the kitchen island, each holding a mug of coffee that had gone cold. Their energy was gone, replaced with a bone-deep, numbing exhaustion. But sleep wouldn't come to them for hours yet.

Every door and window in the house was locked, and the gun Rey had fired rested at his left side within arm's reach. Thankfully, Sierra hadn't seen the Dogman, just her father's truck sliding through their backyard and

Daddy firing a gun at the tree line. She was confused and scared because her parents were scared, but she wouldn't have the same haunting nightmares that would plague Rey for years to come.

He told Felicia everything. From the first time he met Frank to lowering the gun with the barrel still hot. At first, she didn't want to listen and rejected every word he said. But there was no other explanation for what she had seen with her own eyes. Wishing it didn't exist didn't stop it from existing. And attacking.

"You could take Sierra and go to your mom's house," Rey offered, breaking the thick silence.

Slowly, she raised her eyes from the top of the mug to her husband.

"And what about you? Aren't you coming, too?"

Rey hunched forward with a heavy sigh.

"I can't just quit this job. I'll never get my old position back. We spent everything on this house. I'll stay here and work for a few months, take as much from each paycheck as we can and save it up, then we can move somewhere else. We'll probably have to go back to living in an apartment, but we'll make it work until we can rebuild ourselves," he mumbled.

"You would stay here with that thing out there?" she hissed.

He looked up at her pointedly. "I have the gun."

"And it ran faster than your truck!"

"I'll be safe."

Felicia slammed her fists down on the counter. "You

can't promise that!"

"Then what would you have me do! We have no savings and no job to fall back on. What are we supposed to do, Felicia!" Rey snapped back.

Her lips pressed into a thin line, her green eyes glossing with unshed tears before she looked away.

"I don't know," she whispered. "But I don't want to lose you. I can't lose you."

Rey shook his head, staring back down into his mug.

"This was supposed to be our dream."

Felicia reached over and peeled his hand away, threading her fingers through his.

"My dream is to grow old with you and watch Sierra live a happy and healthy life. This"—she motioned around with her other hand—"was nice but it means nothing if we aren't alive to enjoy it."

He gave her hand a gentle squeeze.

"There has to be some way to fight this thing. Someone else must have met it before and lived through it. If we could fight back, then we could have both dreams come true."

The silence settled around them again. The gun was a good weapon, but knowledge was worth more. They were in a corner with no way out. Not unless that stunt earlier scared the creature off for good, but Rey doubted that. It would hide for tonight but come for them again later.

"Actually, we might have something," Felicia mumbled so quietly that Rey wasn't sure he heard her right.

"What?"

She released his hand and slid off the stool. Her legs were still shaky, making her grab onto the counter for a moment before shuffling towards the stairs.

"I found a book earlier in that old desk. It might be nothing but . . ." She trailed off as Rey's eyes slowly widened.

"It could be about the Dogman," he finished.

She nodded and led the way to the office.

"Why didn't you tell me about this sooner?" he asked.

"I had forgotten about it. It was exciting but being attacked by something straight out of a cheesy horror flick kind of took more precedence," she muttered back with an eye roll.

Rey ducked his head sheepishly as they approached the trapdoor.

"Ah, right. Sorry about that."

She waved his apology off as he unlocked the door and lowered the ladder. Again, she went first and climbed through the hole to the attic. When her knees were pressed firmly into the floorboards, she reached into her pocket and turned on the flashlight app. The space illuminated in a blue hue as Rey pulled himself up beside her. They stood and walked carefully over to the desk where she knelt and opened the bottom drawer, drawing out the thick leather journal with bright red ribbon around it.

"I think the ribbon has to be cut. I couldn't get the

knot undone when I found it, but we might get some answers to our issue inside."

Rey nodded as he carefully turned the book in his hands. There were no significant markings on either side of the journal. Honestly, it could contain anything. Cooking recipes, the angsty poetry of a teenager, love letters from the war . . .

But for the first time in a few hours, Rey felt hope again.

CHAPTER TWENTY-ONE

THEY SAT back around the kitchen island with a glass of wine and a pair of scissors. For a moment as she poured it, Felicia felt guilty drinking when her daughter could wander out of bed at any second. But sometimes wine was necessary. Like when unsealing an old mysterious book that might contain vital information about a myth come to life.

Rey did the honors and snipped the ribbon next to the tight knot. The fabric floated away and they both leaned closer as he carefully opened the front cover. The leather cracked as it moved, making both of them cringe. The paper inside was yellowed and the ink was so faded that the first few pages were damn near illegible.

Rey made an irritated sound and started carefully flipping through the book.

"What are you doing?" Felicia asked with a raised brow.

"The good stuff is always at the end of books, so I'm skipping to the end," he muttered, deep in concentration. The last entry was slightly past the middle of the book. The handwriting was neat and clear in thick, black ink without a date or signature to let them know who had written it.

The Dogman was said to appear in a ten-year cycle that falls on years ending in seven. It stands seven or eight feet tall with the torso of a man and head of a canine-like beast. The fearsome howl of the beast can be heard for miles, sometimes sounding like a human scream—a pained scream.

He will not stop until he gets revenge. IT is coming! Be prepared!

Rey paused, reading the passage again and flipping back a page to see if he missed something.

"Ah, just kidding. The end of the book is a creepy Wikipedia entry. Your turn."

He slid the book over to his wife who just shook her head and turned back further. Her eyes skimmed over the writing as she made her way back to the beginning of the book.

"All of these entries are written by different people," she mumbled.

"How do you know? Barely any of them had a name signed," he asked, taking a sip of his wine.

She tipped the book towards him for a moment before continuing her search.

"The handwriting is different. The ink is different. And the dates are about ten years apart," she stated.

"I guess the creepy Wiki was right about that at least," he muttered.

"Which is good. That means this thing hibernates, and we can relax while it does. I just wish someone said why and when it does it . . ."

Rey nodded as she paused at an entry with a frown. A minute ticked by, then two when he finally asked what was wrong. She swallowed thickly before showing him the passage.

August 16, 1987

The creature is like nothing I've ever seen before. I never believed the stories. They were all told by the insane. But insanity saw the truth. The Dogman is real. He came through my backyard and killed my dog. The corpse left in ribbons across the grass. I can't bear it. Poor Lucy didn't deserve it.

I shot the damn monster, but it left with a human scream that I'll never forget. I'm not moving. I refuse to be chased away by a beast. Next time when it comes back, I'll be ready. I have a loaded shotgun and God on my side.

This is America. We fight fo

The rest of the writing was smeared in rust brown stains that soaked through the next few pages and stopped in the last loop of an *O*.

"You're kidding me . . . I think I know who wrote that," Rey gasped out.

"How?"

"I saw the newspaper article. It was thirty years ago and about a man named Aaron Fuller. I thought he was the last person who lived here," he muttered.

Felicia bit her bottom lip and flipped to the next entry with flowery cursive spelling out the horrors of meeting a dog-like beast in the woods.

"I guess he wasn't," she murmured.

"Going through this whole thing is going to take a while," Rey observed as he took a gulp from his glass. Felicia shushed him as she scanned over more of the entries, skipping back further in time.

As the time ticked by, Rey pulled out his phone and started typing away at the screen. He leaned on the island, propping his head up with his left hand while the right slowly scrolled through a website.

"You know what confuses me the most," Rey drawled, irritating his wife with another disruption.

"What?" she grumbled, picking up her glass and taking a sip of the wine.

"All of these stories online say that the Dogman isn't violent. Apparently, they just appear and then disappear when they see people. So, what's the problem with this one? Why did we get the short end of the Dogman stick?"

Felicia sighed, putting the book down with the ribbon tucked between the pages as a marker, and rubbed her face.

"I don't know. A few of these passages say this place is cursed. Maybe that's why he is angry."

"It's mad about a curse? Or it is cursed?"

"Could be either one. I don't know, Rey. This damn thing wasn't supposed to exist to begin with. How am I supposed to know its motives? Maybe he just likes how people taste," she huffed in exacerbation.

He watched her for a moment then glanced at the clock.

"It's getting late, do you want to go to bed and try this again in the morning?" he asked softly.

She covered her face with her hands, breathing through her fingers.

"I don't know if I can. Rey, this is too much. A dog-like creature is hunting us. Our daughter's dolls are possessed." Felicia paused, slowly drawing her hands down her face and dropping them onto the counter. "How are we supposed to figure all of this out and fight it? What are we supposed to do?"

"Wait, what do you mean the dolls are possessed?"

Felicia was silent for a moment as she picked up her

glass and took a long drink from it. Rey watched her intently, his lips thin with stress. Every time he thought they had a lock on the situation something new popped up before his eyes. She was right, it was becoming too much.

"Before I saw that *thing*," she muttered with a shiver. "I was in Sierra's room cleaning up. I . . . I was going through and sorting her toys when I noticed the dolls inside the tiny house were in the same positions that Sierra and I were in. My doll was in the bedroom, and Sierra's doll was in the living room. Then . . ."

Felicia paused, groaned under her breath as she looked up to the ceiling.

"I don't know. I forgot what exactly happened, but I saw the doll move! My doll turned and looked right at me, Rey! Then that ugly doll we burned—the Dogman replica—was right outside of the tiny house."

"It's back? It can't be back. Felicia, we burned that thing to ash! When did this happen?" he gasped out.

"Don't patronize me! I know what I saw," she snapped, sliding off her stool. "And it happened about five minutes before you barreled through the backyard like a bat out of hell," she muttered back. She took a few long strides around the counter towards the hall, pausing to looking at his gawking expression with a scowl.

"Come on, I'll show you it."

Rey shook his head, slowing rising from his seat.

"This is unbelievable," he muttered, trailing

behind her.

"Everything since we've moved in has been unbelievable," she retorted with a snort as she pulled open Sierra's bedroom door. She stepped into the dark, flipping on the light switch and waving her hand towards the tiny house in the middle of the floor.

"See?"

Rey stepped beside her, scanning the floor and few toys still littering the area.

"Hate to break it to you, babe, but I don't see anything." He scoffed, kicking a polka dotted sock out of his way.

"You've got to be kidding me!"

CHAPTER TWENTY-TWO

"I SWEAR, Rey, it was right here!" she gasped, pointing next to the dollhouse at the empty floor. She walked around the entire structure, her eyes flicking from one spot to another on the ground. But he was right. The doll wasn't there.

Rey crouched before the dollhouse, peering into the rooms curiously as Felicia knelt to look under the bed and desk. She let out a sound of distress as the Dogman figurine remained elusive to her hunt. But she was right about the other toys.

The peg doll versions of Rey and Felicia stood inside the replica daughter's room. And Sierra's miniature stood on the wooden version of her parent's bed, facing the dresser where the television would be.

They stood immobile, staring blankly at the walls. However, Rey thought with a deepening frown, their placement was horribly coincidental. Every peg was in nearly the perfect position as their live counterpart should be. Though both parent pegs stood in front of the cardboard dollhouse, and Felicia was actually digging frantically through the closet. And Rey didn't know where Sierra was to say for sure that she was in bed. He loved her dearly, but sometimes she liked to get up and play a little bit before going to sleep.

Was this enough proof to prove what his wife had informed him of earlier? He didn't believe she would lie. However, their stranger than fiction life was becoming overwhelming. He agreed with her statement earlier—it was becoming too much. They had hundreds of questions with no answers. Something needed to give.

"Okay," Rey sighed, rubbing the back of his neck. "It's okay. But is there anything else that happened, or that you found that you forgot to tell me about?"

He held his hand up when Felicia whirled around on her knees to face him. Her eyebrows rose into her hairline and her mouth opened wide to protest.

"I'm not blaming you for forgetting, we didn't know how important the book would be and the attack has us stressed out. But literally anything in this house could be a clue to this whole thing. It could be important to defeating or stopping that creature for another ten years. Or maybe it's another part of the curse that will kill us when our backs are turned. I don't know. But we need to go over it *all*," he explained quickly.

Felicia closed her mouth and nodded, her lips

pulling down as she mulled it over. After a moment she shook her head, small wisps of her hair escaping her bun and falling into her face.

"No, I think this was it."

She paused for a moment, shuffling over on the hardwood floor to peek inside the doll house. The wooden figures remained still.

"I swear they moved, Rey. I saw it. I didn't believe it at first, but I know it happened, "She insisted desperately.

Rey nodded, wrapping an arm around her and pressing a kiss to her temple.

"I believe you, hon," he murmured.

She gave him a flat look but said nothing. Rey gave her another quick kiss before pulling himself up to his feet. He looked down at the toys then turned for the door. There was nothing here that would help them. No clues, no answers. Nothing. They may as well keep poring over the journal for information. Or searching online.

Lost in his thoughts, Rey nearly missed the soft tapping sound as he stepped over the threshold of the bedroom. It was quiet and paused for a long second before making another quick, hushed noise. He froze, turning his head towards the sound.

Tap.

Pause.

Tap.

Pause.

Rey stepped back into the room, eyeing the door as he reached for the handle. Felicia watched him silently, the concern written across her face as he pulled the door away from the wall and peered behind it.

There, a small wooden figurine carved with spiky fur and painted red eyes hopping forward half an inch then pausing. Hopping forward half an inch then pausing.

"Honey, I found that doll you were looking for . . ."

Felicia jumped to her feet, wringing her hands as she stepped up beside him. Rey pushed the door closed, revealing the Dogman doll slowly making its way forward.

"And it's moving. Just like you said," he added.

The figure stopped, slowly spun until it faced the wall, then shuffled forward again. The wooden base tapped on the floorboards as it made its way along the new path. Rey forced his gaze away while swallowing around the lump in his throat. He turned towards the dollhouse once again to see the toys inside dragging themselves into their new positions as well.

The parent pegs now stood right outside the doorway to the hall, staring at the door.

Rey swallowed thickly, lifting his gaze to his beautiful wife who was covering her mouth in shock as the Dogman figurine shuffled and slid across the floor. The toy was undeterred by socks, dolls, and accessories as it jumped and slid around to avoid anything in its path.

"The dolls are moving exactly like we do," he stated quietly.

Felicia's brow furrowed as she darted her eyes between him and the toys in question.

"How much do you want to bet that the little monster figure is moving exactly like that beast outside?" he asked.

"You think it's warning us where the Dogman actually is?" she mumbled back.

Rey nodded, for even as logic warred with the phenomenon in front of him, he had to admit that this figure was nothing short of pure magic. Whatever fueled the wooden figure seemed limitless. It came back to the bedroom after being thrown away. It survived a fire. Now it orchestrated a miniature army into position, playing the scene of the lives of the patrons in this odd house. Perhaps the doll wasn't magic at all. Perhaps it was the log home that weaved some sort of spell on their belongings.

Whatever it was, it may be what they needed to survive the beast. If his theory was right, and he had no reason to believe it was wrong outside of the normal realm of possibility, then they could finally fight back.

"So, what do we do?"

Rey's mouth twisted as he watched the tiny wooden creature spin around again and hop back towards the wall.

"Now," he said slowly, "we need to get Sierra out of here. Then I'm going to set a trap and kill this thing once and for all."

A moment passed in silence as Felicia digested his statement.

"Really? And how are you going to kill a monster that shouldn't exist, and has been terrorizing this specific house for reasons unknown for years? Don't you think other people have tried before? And where on Earth are we going to send Sierra that we won't have to explain a situation that can't be explained—because it shouldn't be possible!" Her voice edged on hysterics as she stared her husband down in utter disbelief.

Rey cracked his neck with a sigh. "We can send her up to my sister's house. You know Monique would love to see Sierra again. Then I'll read that book frontwards and backwards if I have to. Like I said before, someone somewhere has to know something about this creature. Nothing lives forever. There has to be some way to take it down, and I'm going to find it."

"So, the plan is to drop our daughter off with your sister last minute, then use the bedroom to figure out where the Dogman is with only our house as the only indication of direction? This is insane!"

"It's better than nothing," Rey insisted.

Felicia sighed. "All right. Fine, I agree that we need to get Sierra out of here, so let's start by calling your sister. Are you absolutely sure she is going to be okay with this?"

Rey grinned, digging his cellphone out of his pocket.

"I'm positive. Monique could never say no to me.

Especially after her favorite niece was born."

"Sierra is her only niece but whatever. Let's try your crazy plan because I can't think of anything better yet. But Rey," she added as he turned for the bedroom door. He paused and looked back at her.

"Yeah?"

"If I manage to come up with a different plan, we're going to try that first," she added with a scowl.

He flashed her another bright grin. "Sure thing, babe. But grab that doll for the road. I want to test it out."

CHAPTER TWENTY-THREE

"I CAN'T believe Monique let us drop her off without much notice," Felicia admitted as she clutched a blue sneaker box in her lap with her left hand, and the little black journal tightly in her right.

Rey grinned at her briefly before turning his attention back to the road.

"I told you she wouldn't say no. You need to have more faith in me," he teased lightly.

Felicia rolled her eyes but fell back into an uneasy silence, opening the book and flipping back through the pages. Trees flew by the vehicle as Rey navigated the curves of the road to Fayeville. The drive had once been exciting yet nerve-wracking. They believed they were headed towards their dream of a fresh start in their first house. Now, it was tense and nerve-wracking as they made their way back into the den of hell. The creature that was hunting them living somewhere amongst the thick trees of Michigan. The lush greenery and beautifully blooming late flowers misleading tourists and passersby to the horrors hidden in the shadows.

Long talons, glowing amber eyes, and rows of sharp teeth revealed in a deep, vibrating growl. The Dogman wasn't easy to swallow. The myth had come to life and now haunted the Ramseys' every waking moment. The only slight relief came from knowing their daughter was safe for now. They had a week to figure out the mystery of the Dogman and defeat the creature for good. Or move and lose everything they had built for themselves in the process.

The doll they had discovered to warn them of the fearsome creature was trapped in the shoebox, rattling around and banging into the sides as it hopped back and forth. It hadn't stopped moving the entire two-hour drive from Fayeville to Roseville. When Sierra had inquired about the bouncing box, they quickly stumbled out a response about a broken toy that needed to be fixed while they were out.

"Hey, so I think I found something," Felicia started, lifting the book higher to her face as her eyes scanned over the looping script. "This passage is dated August 26, 1927:

This land is cursed with an angry spirit. He hunts once every ten years and feasts on the flesh of man. I cannot move, laid heavy with child. Yet I have seen his mark in the forest. I fear for myself and my babe.

I have sent a message to Kasa to help me. She will know how to hide. I only hope it is not too late. I will continue to pray for guidance.

Then it goes to July 7, 1936 and says:

Kasa has sent me a talisman to warn of the arrival of the beast. He will move as the beast does and warn any of its arrival. Through the Great Spirit we will be saved. I cannot thank her enough for the doll. Though I move on, I shall leave it behind to help the next soul that meets this unkind fate. Listen to the spirits, they will keep you from harm. Gods Bless."

The car slowed as it entered the town, the trees finally giving away to lines of little shops in neat rows along the road. A pastry store, a family-owned restaurant, a barber. Rey looked through the wide expanse of windows boasting the best business in town without taking in much of the details as he mulled the information over.

"I guess that would explain why the Dogman figurine was left at the house. But do you really think this woman knew someone who could put a sort of spell on a toy to warn anyone who has it about the Dogman?"

Felicia shrugged, lowering the book back to her lap as the box wiggled with the bouncing toy in question.

"At this point, I don't see why not. I mean—and I'm getting tired of repeating this—we're being hunted by a myth. I don't know how else to explain the Dogman other than a magical creature come to life. So why wouldn't someone else use magic to try and stop it?"

Rey frowned, flexing his fingers on the steering wheel.

"I suppose you're right, but we're going to be screwed if magic is the only thing that'll work against this thing. Unless," he added teasingly, "you want to suddenly admit to me that you're part witch or something."

Felicia rolled her eyes with a scoff. "No, sorry."

The car stopped at a corner, the brick-and-mortar shops fading back into pure forests dotted with small homes of all different designs. A whitewashed one stood out starkly against its green and brown surroundings. A large wooden sign planted in the middle of the lawn painted white with bold black letters announced, "IT is coming! Be prepared!"

The couple stared for a moment before Rey asked, "Didn't we see that same warning in the book?"

"Do you think it's a coincidence?" Felicia murmured.

Rey glanced up at the rearview mirror before reversing down the road.

"At this point, no, I don't," he muttered darkly as he maneuvered the vehicle into the dirt driveway baring their ominous warning.

He pulled up next to a small gravel lined walkway

and threw the car into park. Felicia tucked the shoebox and book on the floor by her feet as together they unbuckled their seatbelts. The modest sized house had a well-kept lawn, old Toyota pickup truck near the back garage, and curtain drawn windows. From the outside it looked normal, barring the odd sign out front, but nothing seemed to move within the home. A thought tugged at the back of Rey's mind about the home, but he couldn't grasp it. It was familiar in a way beyond their original passing by.

Felicia shot her husband a nervous glance as they exited the vehicle and started down the path, their shoes crunching over the gravel.

"Do you think anyone's home?"

Rey shrugged as they reached the small concrete porch with two cracking steps.

"We're about to find out."

"All right, but let me start the conversation, please. We don't want these people to think we're crazy. The sign could just be a religious statement," she added quietly.

Rey nodded as he lifted his hand to knock on the thick, white paint door. The sound reverberated in the quiet midday, interrupted only by a lone bird high within the trees. A minute passed with no sign of life within the dwelling. Felicia shuffled on the small porch, peering behind her at the deserted road as Rey knocked again.

The longer the silence stretched, the more Felicia

began to doubt this impulsive decision. What were they going to do? Ask what the sign meant and hoped it pertained to their dilemma? Then receive some sage advice that would turn the tides of this mysterious war in their favor so that they could live out their dreams within their lovely new home. It was ridiculous!

She groaned inwardly while running through her lines. *Hello, we're the Ramseys and we're new in town. We just wanted to get to know the neighbors. How are you today?*

No.

Hello, we're new in town and saw your lovely sign. Care to tell us what it's about?

No.

Everything fled from her mind as finally the door creaked open to reveal an older woman with long gray hair piled on top of her head. She was short, coming up to Felicia's chin and wore a long, deep purple dress with a rosary around her neck.

Oh shit, Felicia thought while forcing a smile on her face, *the sign was a religious statement*. She should have known that it was too good to be true.

The woman's brown eyes narrowed in suspicion as she took in the awkward couple. Felicia cleared her throat before offering her hand to the woman.

"Hi! We're the Ramseys and we're new here. I'm Felicia and this is my husband, Rey. We just wanted to come by and meet the neighbors," she greeted with a false note of cheer to her tone.

"Oh? I didn't know the Overtons moved out, or did you take the old Bedford home?" the woman asked, shaking her offered hand then turning to Rey who had his held out as well.

"Uh, neither . . . We actually live down Malberry lane," Felicia admitted as she rubbed the back of her neck.

The woman's eyes narrowed further. "Isn't that a few streets away from here?"

Rey flashed her a smile and a soft chuckle.

"Okay, you got us. We stopped by because your sign caught our eye. It's beautifully crafted, did you make it yourself?"

"I sure did. Only needs to be touched up with some paint every now and then," she boasted, placing one hand on her hip while the other held onto the edge of the door.

Rey nodded, looking back at the sign thoughtfully when it finally hit him. He looked back at the woman with his head cocked as he took her in.

"I used to do some woodworking myself. Have you thought about adding a wishing well to your yard?" he mused.

The woman shook her head. "No, that sign isn't decoration to make my yard look pretty. It's a warning."

"A warning about what?" Felicia piped up, leaning closer to the woman.

Her eyes hardened on the couple as she breathed out, "Nothing you would believe."

She stepped back and started to close the front door. Felicia jerked forward, slamming her palm against the wood to stop her.

"Please, tell us. I can promise you that we're more open-minded than you think," she pleaded. The woman watched her for a moment, her gaze harsh and full of disbelief.

"Please, we need help. Frank said you could help us with something important," Rey added, pressing in behind his wife and crowding the doorway.

The woman sighed, a bone deep exhaustion settling into her features as she slowly opened the door back up and waved them into the house.

"Frank? Fine, come in and have a seat. But I'm telling you now, most of the town here thinks I'm crazy, and if you are here to try and play some kind of joke on me, I won't be forgiving!"

Felicia smiled in relief, stepped into the small entryway with a curious glance at her husband. Rey simply rubbed her back and ushered her further into the house.

"I promise we would never do that," he promised.

The woman nodded and waved them towards a green couch covered in floral print in the simple but small living room. They took a seat as she introduced herself as Laura Virgo and offered to fetch them some water or tea. They waved her offer off politely and settled into the plush cushions with throw pillows decorated with handstitched sunflowers. The walls of the living room were cream with photos hanging up of animals and presumably family members. Across from them was a bare fireplace with an urn on the mantle.

Laura stood in front of it, running a hand down the length of her dress as they took in her home. The living room was attached to the dining room where a small round table with four chairs took up most of the wooden floor. The kitchen was just a short hall with barely enough room for two people to stand shoulder to shoulder, and on the other side of the living room was a small hallway with three closed doors.

"Tell me exactly where you live down Malberry," she started.

"8893—it's a log house off of the road there. Do you know that house?" Felicia replied.

Laura nodded somberly. "Of course, I do. My best friend used to live there. His name was Aaron Fuller."

CHAPTER TWENTY-FOUR

"**AARON WAS** a sweet man but more stubborn than a mule. We were young at the time, and madly in love. He was my best friend, my fiancé, my everything. We were going to get married the following year and were planning a big wedding in the next town over. He had gotten that house for us, and everything was going just right in our lives. Then, it appeared." She paused with a shiver.

"A monster not from this world. When he first told me about the beast, I thought he was joking. Then it attacked poor little Lucy—his dog—and I was shattered. Nobody would believe Aaron about the beast, so he planned to catch it and show the whole town. I remember one night I had snuck off to see him because I was worried about how he was handling his grief. I saw the creature with my own eyes, lurking in the trees in the backyard.

"Aaron was furious and kept a loaded gun in almost every room of the house. He said he wasn't going to let a werewolf keep us from our dreams. He was going to get revenge for Lucy and give me the house I deserved. Then . . ." her voice wavered. "Then it killed him. Right in the middle of the day with a rifle by his side."

"Even after seeing the damage the creature had done to Aaron, nobody would believe me about what killed him. But you two know, don't you? You've seen it—the Dogman," she stated.

The Ramseys exchanged a look before nodding to Laura.

"Yeah, we've seen it. Did you write that last passage in the journal?" Felicia inquired quietly.

"I found it after . . . Well, you know. At first, I was going to keep it. It was the last thing he did. But I read through the other passages and knew that I had to put it back. I needed to keep warning everyone about the Dogman before the same fate befell another innocent person. I made that sign shortly after it, too. I've done just about everything I could think of to warn everyone away from that place."

Felicia shifted in her seat. "What is the Dogman exactly? Why does he exist and why is he hunting anyone that lives in that house?"

"Yeah, from everything I read the Dogman is supposed to be a peaceful creature. This thing is bloodthirsty," Rey added solemnly.

"That's because it's cursed," Laura answered

shortly as she shuffled towards the hallway. The couple watched her disappear around the corner, the sound of a door opening drifting out to them in the growing silence.

A moment later she reappeared with another thick black book with papers jutting out from odd places within the pages. It was held together by a metal clasp that had seen better days. She twisted the clasp open as she walked towards them and carefully opened the journal. Inside was looping handwriting and newspaper clippings taped to the pages. She scanned the contents, turning over the pages until she got to what she was searching for and handed it over with a nod.

It was a photocopy of a torn diary page, but the image was manipulated so the background was pitch black with the writing impressions light gray. It was dated for 1917.

"This looks kind of familiar," Rey noted.

Laura chuckled.

"It should. I copied the first eight pages of the journal before I returned it to the house. You can't read them as they are in the book, but I managed to figure out the right settings to make them stand out on a computer." She paused and sniffed. "Well, it might not be the best job, but it certainly worked well enough. And this tells about the Dogman, and the woman whose curse gave him life."

"Her name was Malora Hail, and she used to be a midwife back in the early 1900s. She had a dog whom she cared for deeply named Nora gifted to her by her father when she was a child. Now, keep in mind Fayeville was small back then. Heck, I'm not even sure that was the original name of the town. At the time it had only a hundred residents, but it was surely growing, thanks to the mining industry.

"She detailed her life in her journal from about ten years of age—although I am just guessing on that. Most of it was lived happily with her mother and father in this small town until she hit puberty and started being courted by the men in the area. She says very quickly that she felt hunted like an animal, and viewed as livestock instead of an individual. After her parents died from illness, the attention got worse. So much so that she began fearing for her safety.

"She never left without her dog with her, she kept her visitation with the residents of Fayeville as minimal as possible, but unfortunately it wasn't enough. She had a few bad run ins with some suitors who weren't taking her polite no as an answer. One of those suitors isn't referred to by name, however, the attention became so bad that she ended up striking him when he attempted to grab her arm and presumably pull her away to his home.

"She says he threatened her upon walking away, promising retribution for her attack. Either he would have her as his bride, or she would disappear."

July the 25th

149

He spat out a vile, evil curse as he walked away. By the weeks end I must become his bride and accept the consequences of striking him or He promises more than death. He promises annihilation. And neither man nor animal would see my face. Not tree, stone, nor wind would whisper my name. My soul will blink out before reaching the Heavens.

And I believe him.

I must do something about this. I do not want to be forgotten. I do not want to die. I want to live.

"Malora discusses shadows watching her outside of her windows, and Lemaul barking in the middle of the night at the trees outside. She was so concerned about it that near the end of her entries she talks about casting a spell to protect herself from harm."

Laura paused to flip the pages over until two sentences were blown up and highlighted on another dark and grainy image.

Man lived with dirt until dirt became mud. One hundred and ten and seven and so two became one.

"She was a witch?" Felicia clarified softly, passing

the journal over for her husband to see.

Rey stared at the words with a sharp intake of breath. He had seen that page before. Torn and worn down, he'd disregarded it and tossed the piece of paper aside. It was still in the attic, resting on top of one of the boxes of seasonal decorations and covered in a fine layer of dust by now.

"Yes. It took me forever to research the ritual she was performing because she doesn't discuss every step she took during the casting—and some pages of the journal were missing. However, I believe with the information present that she was trying to summon a guardian to her side to aid her against enemies.

"Obviously, it didn't go as planned. The last page of the diary spoke about running out of time as the hunters drew near. She wasn't just afraid, she was angry. Angry at the townspeople for turning a blind eye towards the behavior she was receiving. Angry at her parents for leaving her unprepared for the harsh world around her. Angry at herself for ignoring the signs for so long.

"So rather than opening the gate and pulling a creature out to help her, she created one of her own. A beast that would stand beside her no matter what and kill anyone who came near her without consent. It was that night that they attacked.

"On August 1st, 1917, Malora Hail and everything she had owned disappeared in a massive blaze. And the world forgot that she existed."

A silence settled over the group as they digested the

information. Rey and Felicia exchanged uncomfortable looks, each shifting slightly in their seat.

"So," Rey started slowly, "the Dogman was meant to be a guardian of sorts to protect Malora, but the spell was finished too late to save her? So now it wanders around killing people who live on our property every ten years . . ." His voice trailed off.

"It's still trying to protect her, even after she died," Felicia murmured.

Laura nodded sadly. "It was too late to keep her alive but continues to stand dutifully by her side in death. This has become a curse for the people who live here but was only meant to finally free an innocent woman from constant threat."

"That means she has to be near the house somewhere. If she was afraid of disappearing from existence, all we have to do is find her and let her know that she hasn't been forgotten," Rey murmured.

"She is buried in an unmarked grave, otherwise it would have been done before," Laura sighed. "I've searched every record in our library and online that I could find about Malora Hail. Nobody knows anything about this poor girl."

"What about following the footprints? He left a pretty good impression in the backyard after it rained . . ." Felicia mused.

Laura shook her head. "Several folks have tried to track him in the past. The footprints always disappear shortly into the forest."

"That all may be true, but thanks to another family we now have magic on our side," Rey said slowly, his eyes lighting up as he jumped to his feet. "Babe, we need to get a map of the area and a couple quick supplies. We're going to hunt the Dogman."

CHAPTER TWENTY-FIVE

THE DOOR to the hardware shop chimed as Felicia and Rey filed in. Frank stood behind the front counter in a red and yellow plaid shirt, smiling as the couple paused in the doorway. The warm glow of the light panels bathed everything in gold and reflected off the freshly mopped tiled floor.

"Hey, Frank! Good to see you again," Rey greeted, striding over to shake the man's hand.

Frank's face crinkled with laugh lines as he chuckled and returned the sentiment.

"What brings ya back here? Looking for more traps or somethin'?" he asked, looking over at Felicia. "And is this yer wife that ya spoke so highly about?" he added with a wink.

Rey chuckled, tucking Felicia under his arm as she drew near.

"She sure is, I don't know how I was lucky enough

to keep her, though. Felicia, this is Frank. Frank, meet my wife, Felicia."

The two exchanged polite greetings as Rey scanned the front of the store.

"I hate to cut this short, but we were looking for some large cement blocks, or maybe brick pavers. Do you have anything like that around?"

Frank's expression darkened as he quickly glanced at the door to make sure they would be alone. His voice lowered as he leaned closer. "Of course. Does this have anything to do with your problem in the backyard?"

Rey nodded. "Yeah, we think we know how to break the curse of that creature."

The older man shuffled out from behind the counter and led them down the last aisle in the store. His shoes squeaked slightly as he walked with one hand bracing his lower back.

"Now I don't have a large selection to buy from on hand, but the samples are over here, and I can order whatever quantity you need online. It'll be delivered straight to your doorstep, if you would like," Frank offered as he waved to a display tucked between gardening supplies and renovation tools.

The display was bright white with chunks of stone, cement, and brick laid on top of a metal counter. Information about each type of paver and how to install it hung on the back of the display case with a small booklet with services to install a patio walkway locally.

"I only need one brick, or slab of stone."

Frank cocked a brow and tilted his head as he observed the sample selection again. Rubbing his chin thoughtfully, he picked up a large piece of gray speckled stone and turned it in his palms to inspect the surface. It was shaped like a rectangle with rounded corners and a few chips around the side.

"Only one? What for?"

"We're going to make a tombstone with it. We believe that the Dogman exists to protect a young woman who was threatened with total annihilation. We can't give her back her life, but we can let her know that she is still remembered and that the threat to her is over. We're going to try and give her peace now."

"She doesn't have a grave already?"

Felicia shook her head sadly, wringing her hands as Rey recounted what they knew about Malora Hail. Frank listened with rapt attention, his gaze never wavering from them as the details came pouring out. A young woman whose life was ended too soon, and her body tossed away into the unknown without anyone to mourn the loss.

They didn't understand exactly how the magic worked and could debate whether or not the Dogman was a demon pulled from the gates of Hell. It still stood that their best weapon against the lingering darkness of Malora's untimely death wasn't holy water but empathy. Like anyone else, she deserved to be treated as a human and given the basic rights that everyone else was afforded. She needed to know she wasn't alone, even in death.

"I don't agree with leavin' the thing alive, but if it'll help, just take it. I can always order more. Should probably replace these anyway, they're lookin' dingy from everyone touching them."

Rey took the stone with wide eyes. Felicia's hands fluttered near her mouth as her eyes regarded the older man softly.

"Frank, we would be more than happy to pay. You don't have to do this," Rey offered, tucking the object into the crook of his elbow as he dug in his back pocket for his wallet.

Frank waved him off. "As I said, anything I can do to help you with your problem I will. And this gets me to tidy up this display. So, does the creature only come out at night or somethin'? How are you gonna stay safe during this whole thing?"

Rey's lips turned down as he glanced at his wife. This was the part of the plan they didn't necessarily agree on. Since the Dogman attacked once during the day, they couldn't be completely sure it wouldn't still be wandering through the forest when they hunted it down. Heck, they couldn't guarantee it wasn't sitting at the house, waiting for them to pull up right this moment. Everything hinged on hope and luck.

"It doesn't seem to operate under any specific hours, so if we see him, I'm going to distract him and give Felicia the time she needs to find Malora."

"You're not gonna do that alone," Frank stated with his jaw set.

Rey shook his head. "I can't let you be a part of this, too, Frank. Too many lives are going to be risked as it is. I'm not adding yours to the list."

The old man scoffed. "Just let me worry about that. I may be old, but I'm not incompetent. You're gonna need backup to go against something that defies the laws of nature. This creature . . . You've read about what it's done. You think it won't do that to you because you're young? Well, let me reassure you that you're wrong. It'll tear ya up and spit ya out faster than you could call for help."

"Which is exactly why I can't let you do this. I don't want to bury friends."

"And ya think I do?"

Felicia watched as the guys stood off against one another silently, their eyes locked in determination and shoulders pulled back. A minute ticked by before Frank sighed in defeat. His shoulders sagged slightly as he regarded the couple carefully.

"All right, fine. But call me if anything happens. I want to know y'all make it safe out of this mess. And if ya change your mind, I'll be free to help in any way that I can."

Rey relaxed and nodded with a soft smile.

"Of course. Thank you again for everything. This means a lot to us."

"Say nothing of it. It's what friends are for."

CHAPTER TWENTY- SIX

LAURA INSISTED on helping until the very end, and unlike Frank, she wouldn't budge no matter what. With the death of her dear beloved, she had a stake in seeing the spell finally broken and receiving closure. Felicia had given her directions to the house and they parted ways to break down the supply list needed to pull the tentative plan off.

A stone and paint for a tombstone, flowers to leave at the grave per Felicia's request, the gun in case things didn't pan out well, a map of the area, walkie-talkies, and a shovel that rested in the Ramseys' garage to help plant the stone.

They headed back to the property, the book and figurine resting by Felicia's feet, in relative silence. The job was simple but so much rested on this one action working that the tension was still palpable in the air. They had met some amazing people to help them set their lives straight and flush out the threat against them. They could say with utmost certainty that without these important lifelines, they would be forced to lose everything close to them to this monster lurking outside their door.

And it was because of that, that they weren't sure whether to call this Dogman a curse or not. If it had not been for the creature, would they be this close to Frank? Would they have discovered what a passionate and caring person Laura was? Having a close family tended to create a bubble that was easy to live inside of for days, weeks, even years. At the apartment, Felicia could name maybe three other residents, and they sure didn't speak to one another besides asking about rent changes or barking orders to be quieter on the weekends.

If they could solve the mystery of the Dogman, this move would be exactly as they imagined when they first browsed for a new home. It was a warm and friendly community with great opportunities for Sierra's future.

As the car pulled up the long, winding driveway they prepared themselves for the final showdown. If this didn't work, then they would have to move. That was if they managed to escape the Dogman alive.

Felicia took an extra moment to study her husband. A twinge of panic slid down her spine at the thought of possibly losing him. She wouldn't be able to recover from the loss. And what about Sierra? How would she be able to cope with the death of one of her parents? So much could go wrong—would most likely go wrong. It was a suffocating thought.

Rey watched her with his own darkened gaze. He reached out slowly and picked her hand up from on her lap, caressing her fingers with a light brush of his thumb. His smile was weak, but the gesture helped to sooth her growing nerves.

"It'll be all right, baby. I promise," he murmured.

"How can you promise that?" she croaked out in the stifling air of the rapidly shrinking vehicle.

"Because there is no other option. We're not going to lose each other, or this house. I won't let that happen. Trust me, okay? We'll make it out of this just fine." His tone left no room for argument. Come hell or high water, Rey would see to it that they emerged from that forest together.

They exited the car and began the short walk to the front door, pausing only to unlock the door as the gravel behind them crunched under the tires of another car. Felicia spun around to wave as Laura pulled up behind their vehicle while Rey ducked inside.

The older woman climbed out with an answering grin, pausing to dig a large deep purple purse out from the passenger seat and a bright white grocery bag. She slammed the door behind her and locked it while wandering up the wooden steps of the porch.

"Great timing, Laura. And thank you again for helping us."

She waved the comment off, hitching the purse

higher on her shoulder as they stepped inside the house.

"Thank you for letting me do so. Aaron meant the world to me—still does. It'll be good to see the thing that murdered him finally leave this Earth for good."

Rey stood by the kitchen island, dumping his keys and wallet on the smooth granite top.

"Let's head to Sierra's room. That's where the dolls are. With whatever magic moves these things, we should be able to find this grave pretty quickly."

"Dolls?" Laura asked, shifting the grocery bag so Felicia could pass her by down the short hall without bumping into the objects inside.

Felicia nodded, her expression blank as Rey opened their daughter's bedroom door.

"Yeah, I guess awhile back someone got ahold of these dolls to tell her where the Dogman was so she could hide from him. We found them inside the tiny house replica when we first moved in, but they were pretty much blank canvases. So, I painted them to look like us as a gift for our daughter and now they show us where we're standing in the house."

"The entire thing is really odd, but it works. Trust us," Rey added.

Felicia stepped forward to the pink room but paused at the doorway as she surveyed the floor.

"One quick question, babe. Where is the little girl?"

For a moment Felicia stood frozen in the door, staring down at the dollhouse in the middle of a pink area rug. The parents' dolls stood in the hall of the house, staring into the little girl's room, but the last doll was missing from the collection.

Rey gently nudged her further into the room, sitting down slightly off to the side of the opened back of the replica as the other two filed in behind him.

"I told you, it's magic. The doll probably popped into another dimension or something when Sierra left the town," he explained with a shrug.

Laura slowly lowered herself the floor on the other side of the tiny house as Felicia carefully stepped around them to drop down in front of a small white desk, making a loose circle of bodies around the dollhouse. Then Felicia opened the shoebox and brought out an ugly carved beast.

For a few minutes, all Laura could do was stare as the toy suddenly wiggled with life. When it was been placed down, the couple feared she would faint. Her face went white as the figure hopped around the rug then beelined to the wall by the door where it began restlessly moving back and forth. But she took it in stride and recomposed herself quickly.

"Amazing," was the only thing she breathed out before diving into the task at hand, distributing various items from the grocery bag to the others.

She pulled out a map of the area and laid it on the floor carefully, smoothing the folded edges to sit flat for them to pore over. Felicia pushed fresh batteries into three walkie-talkies as Rey measured out the distance from the Dogman toy to the dollhouse.

"The Dogman figure is currently five feet and three quarter inches south of the dollhouse," Rey mumbled, retracting his tape measure. Laura noted the measurement within the black journal as Felicia stood up and dusted off her knees.

"Okay, let me know if he moves closer to our property line. I'll head out to the backyard." Felicia turned on the walkie-talkie, nodding to Laura as she did the same with a spare and marched out of the bedroom.

For a moment, the mommy peg remained immobile within the house. The soft click of the sliding glass door reached them before the doll finally came to life. It slowly moved across the floors towards the back door. The phenomenon was as interesting as it was disturbing. Rey could almost convince himself that the Dogman figure was battery operated; but watching as the doll depicting his wife moved along the same path through the house that she did was something else.

He couldn't not believe it was magic, and that unnerved the logical side of himself that protested the existence of the creature outside.

The doll came to the back door area, a closed wall within the dollhouse with a piece of paper glued up to reflect the sliding glass doors. At first it simply hopped headfirst into the wall and slid back slightly. Rey frowned, wondering briefly if he should move the peg around the wall himself. Then with a soft almost inaudible pop, the doll disappeared and reappeared next to the home. It continued to hop along the unseen track slowly until finally coming to a stop near the edge of the rug.

The radio clicked on with Felicia's voice cracking through the soft hiss of static.

"Okay, I'm here."

Rey measured the distance then called out, "one foot" so Laura could jot the numbers down. She waited for him to nod in satisfaction before picking up the walkie-talkie and radioing back.

"Perfect, come on back."

"Gotcha, be there in a minute!"

Rey frowned at the tape measure, leaning over to review the information recorded in the journal.

"We have roughly an acre of land. The backyard is most of it, so the Dogman is about 24,000 yards away from where we're sitting now. How have we missed seeing this thing pace around?" he wondered aloud.

"I don't want to pester, but your math is off. Regardless, the trees are thicker than you realize, and the Dogman isn't exactly south of us. Nor is it exactly 24,000 yards away because you measured five feet and three-quarter inches," Laura pointed.

"Even still," he grumbled quietly while rubbing the back of his head. "That isn't on our property. I think that belongs to someone else, so why is it coming here?"

"It used to belong to the Hail family until the massive fire wiped everything out. Then the land was divided and resold. Part of the land was bought by the state, which is where I believe we are headed. No worries, it isn't heavily guarded or anything. But if you want to purchase more land, it will cost an arm and a leg to do so," Laura informed him as she pored over the map.

"Glad to know I won't likely be caught trespassing," Rey mumbled as the bedroom door opened and his wife slipped back inside.

"Did it work? Do we know where the Dogman is?" she asked, slightly out of breath.

Rey sighed, leaning back and tipping his head up as she bent over him to drop a quick kiss on his lips.

"We have an idea on where to start searching," Laura said with a smile. She shuffled around to circle an area on the map with a red pen.

Felicia's face brightened up. "Good, then let's do this!"

Rey looked at the window with a slight frown. "I want to get this over with as well, but it's about to be dark out. I don't think it's a good idea to wander around without the sun to help us see where we're stepping."

Laura nodded, recapping the pen and tucking it away into her pocket.

"Then we can look for the grave tomorrow. It'll be better to start early in the morning refreshed, anyway. And it'll give that rock more time to dry," she stated with a nod towards the makeshift tombstone. "And of course, you two are more than welcome to spend the night at my home. It isn't much, but it'll keep you both safe until we can finally give Malora peace."

Rey blinked in surprise. "Are you sure?"

"We couldn't possibly put you out like that," Felicia added quickly.

Laura waved them off, pulling herself to her feet and grabbing her large bag.

"Nonsense! It would be needlessly dangerous to stay here while it's wandering about. This will save you money on a hotel. And I'm not using up that spare room anyway." She paused with a raised brow. "Unless you two were going to chance the Dogman coming through tonight?"

"Well, if you're sure," Felicia murmured slowly, looking down at Rey to see him staring intently at the window again.

"Absolutely. You two get packed and paint up our tombstone really quick. I'll head back to start some dinner. You remember where I live, so finding me shouldn't be an issue. I'll see you both in about an hour!"

Laura slipped out the door before they could argue further, the sounds of her hurried footsteps trailing through the hall and living room. For a moment, Felicia and Rey simply stayed immobile. Both too stunned to react. Then Rey chuckled and broke the silence. He swept up to his feet and spun around to embrace his wife, burying his face in her thick hair.

"What a crazy day," he mumbled.

She laughed, wrapping her arms around him and holding him close.

"It's been a crazy . . . month? Almost a month now?"

Rey took a deep breath before pulling back enough to gaze into her eyes.

"Yeah, I think it's been about a month. Time sure flies, doesn't it?"

She nodded, giving him a quick kiss before pulling away.

"It does. It also feels like we've been here longer than that. This whole thing has just been . . ."

"Crazy?" Rey supplied with a quirk of his lips.

"Definitely. But thankfully we've met some wonderful people to help us with this."

"Yeah. Soon this whole thing will be over and simply a wild memory," he mused.

"Before we leave, I'm going to call Monique and talk to Sierra. I hope she's doing all right. The nightmares seemed to stop, but . . . I don't know. I just need to hear her voice. I can't wait to find normal here." Felicia sighed as stepped outside the door, pulling out her cellphone and flipping through the contacts.

"Me too, baby. Me too."

CHAPTER TWENTY-SEVEN

THE MORNING air was chilly as the group walked up the driveway of the Ramsey residence. Everyone was dressed in jeans, long sleeved shirts, and sturdy shoes. Felicia had her hair pulled back tightly while Laura pushed her hair back with a black band.

Rey hitched a small blue backpack further up his shoulders, the bottom of the bag sagging down to his hips. The map was tucked into his back pocket as they made their way over the gravel to the grass of the backyard. The black shiny tailgate of the pickup truck still waited near the trees; the yard torn from the tires that had slid through the terrain in a gallant effort to protect his family.

"You forgot to move the truck back," Felicia remarked absentmindedly.

Rey shrugged, hitching the backpack higher again in the process. "I forgot about it during this whole fiasco."

"How did you forget about that hulking machine?" Laura asked with a quirk of her brow.

"Material things don't mean anything compared to the safety of my family . . ." His loving words were belittled by the sudden howl of grief Rey belted out when near the vehicle.

The truck's windshield was smashed in with a large, eight-point buck's severed head. A small swarm of flies buzzed around the decaying remains, the pungent stench burning their noses from several feet back.

Blood from the shredded neck dried on the hood of the car in a rust-colored pool that was nearly indecipherable from the paint job. The long drips of the innocent creature slipped down the sides of the vehicle and dried in matted splotches on the grass, with a gory trail leading deep into the woods. Tiny shards of glass glittered on the ground, blinking a warning as they approached the scene.

Rey rushed ahead of the women, darting left and right to survey the damage. His hands fluttered and clenched at his sides. Finally, he whipped around to face the others, pointing at the mangled deer. His face was bright red, the veins popping along his temples as he bellowed, "What the fuck!"

Felicia opened her mouth and then closed it as her husband continued his tirade.

"What the fuck is this! Why? What was the point! Son of a bitch!"

Laura covered her mouth at the destruction. A

nervous laugh bubbled up inside her chest. If the creature could rip the head from a strong, healthy deer then what would it do to them? She swallowed thickly, pushing the dark thought away and attempting to recompose herself.

"I swear to God, we're killing this damn thing now!" he roared, drawing a sharp gasp from his wife.

"Rey!" she scolded as he went back to circling his truck. "What happened to 'material items mean nothing compared to your family?'"

"I didn't know it destroyed my truck! Look at this! It wasn't protecting anything by fucking smashing out my damn window!"

"We can buy a new truck," she pointed out over his string of curses and threats to the Dogman.

"And who is supposed to clean this up? Who am I supposed to call about a severed fucking head! Shit!" Rey kicked something on the ground as he turned his back to the mess, combing his fingers roughly through his short hair.

"We will figure it out, but right now we need to focus! If we don't get this done, your truck will be the least of our problems, remember?" Felicia snapped.

Rey growled and muttered something underneath his breath before turning to face the women. With one more heavy sigh, he finally let the anger ebb enough to return to the mission. He nodded towards the grass and grumbled, "Watch your step. Tons of glass around here." Then he spun on his heels and marched towards the forest line.

Felicia and Laura glanced at one another with mutual shivers before carrying on. The overgrown brush had been crushed down, creating a clear path the veered towards the right. A trail of gore accompanied broken branches and bramble along the way. Large, heavy footprints with claws dug into the earth—far too big to be a dog or coyote. Rey eyed them with bitter rage, his hands flexing at his sides.

"Rey," Felicia started softly, placing her hand on his shoulder. He didn't meet her gaze, shrugging off her touch as they continued searching for the grave. Ignoring the footprints, they followed Laura's compass south, speaking only to call out warnings of rabbit holes and tweaks to their direction.

As time went by, the trees grew denser. The forest closed in on them in a mirrored maze. The uneven ground lending to their slow progression. The tension heating up with each tiny trip across roots or stumbles over rocks. They were elephants storming across the land compared to the relative quiet of the woods. Soon even the soft chirps of the birds and tiny paws of squirrels died off, enveloping them in a disturbing silence.

Felicia's hair stood up as she noted the absence of the mosquitoes that had been following her for the past twenty minutes. The air seemed to grow still around them and heavy with an unnamed force. She shivered, drawing closer to her husband as he slowed his gait with the suddenly changing landscape.

Chunks of rock had broken off, creating jagged cliffs five feet high in front of them. They used moss covered vines to climb the short distance upwards. The high land lasted only another foot before dropping off into a sloped valley, tangled with small broken bushes and crushed wildflowers. Rey slid down the dirt first, then reached back to help Laura and Felicia. Openings of various sizes appeared everywhere around them. Some were obviously abandoned animal dens, covered in overgrown grass and twigs. However, a few appeared large enough to explore with almost squared out entrances and hand-carved walls.

"How much further until we find this thing?" Rey grumbled, adjusting the backpack slightly.

"It has to be close, so be careful," Felicia murmured.

"Then you should take this," he said, sliding the bag off and unzipping the front pocket. He pulled out the gun, double-checking the safety and tucking it in the waist band of his jeans. He grabbed a metal water bottle from the center pocket, nestled in alongside a small shovel and the painted tombstone. He took a long drink before passing it off to Felicia for her to do the same. Laura waved off the offer for her own bottle as she ventured slightly further from their group.

Replacing the bottle in the pack, Felicia hitched it up on her shoulders and adjusted the thick straps until it hung decently comfortable on her back.

"So," Rey started, pulling the gun out and aiming

in at the ground with a tight grip. "If we're close, why don't we see the Dogman yet?"

"Because he isn't up here right now," Laura stated, turning back to face the group near one of the large tunnels.

"He's inside one of the mines. Waiting for us to find him."

CHAPTER TWENTY-EIGHT

"PERFECT. I was afraid this was going to be too easy," Felicia muttered with a roll of her eyes.

"Which tunnel is he in?" Rey rubbed his shoulder absently as he looked around. "This would have been easier if we'd brought the dolls with us. I don't know why we didn't think about that earlier," he added with a huff.

Felicia thought about it for a moment before nodding with a scowl. "Or had someone at the house to watch the dolls move and tell us if we were at least close. How many mine systems are we going to have to check out?"

"I'm more worried about having to dig through rock to get to this body. Or a tunnel collapsing on us while we're down there. This isn't safe."

Laura listened thoughtfully for a moment until a soft rustle nearby made her freeze. The wind picked up loose strands of her hair gently and stirred the leaves, yet something raised the hairs on her arms. A second ticked by, then another. Slowly the tension drained from her shoulders as she cocked her head to listen to nothing.

Nothing.

It was nothing.

Laura opened her mouth to join the discussion as a branch snapped in the bushes a few feet to her right. Everyone froze at the sound. Not a squirrel nor bird in sight, and yet they felt the eyes of something regarding them carefully. Their hearts beat in quick succession as Felicia quietly shuffled closer to her husband. The need to run pounded through Laura's veins as she turned to watch the bush with wide eyes.

The bush wasn't large, only coming up to about her hip, with wide green leaves. Still, another rustle within it sent ice pouring through her veins. The creature lunged.

A small rabbit darted out from the thick branches and sped past Laura's feet in a zig-zagged trail as it wove around their legs and hopped up the sloped hill to safety. When the small furry body finally disappeared, everyone let out a collective breath. It took another moment before Felicia chuckled and Rey sagged.

"Fuck me, I really thought that was the Dogman," he grumbled, drawing a heartier laugh from his wife.

"We all did." She snickered in relief.

Laura quirked a smile, still feeling the edge of

fear prickle her skin. She rubbed her arms against the feeling as she made her way back to the others.

"I guess we aren't as alone as we had thought," she mused.

The comment, though meant to be lighthearted, had everyone peering over their shoulders nervously again.

"We'll just need to keep our eyes open," Rey stated with a slightly awkward chuckle. "No way to avoid going under, though. I guess we should pick a spot and start looking."

"Yeah, it's fine. We'll be fine," Laura added as they started browsing the closest cave entrance. They would have to bend their heads down a little, but the walls inside looked solid. Felicia took out her cellphone and activated the flashlight on it. Slowly, they filed inside.

**

TAP! TAP! *Tap!*

Two wooden pegs slowly hopped across the empty wooden floor, edging closer to the wall. Their black stares fixated on the destination ahead as the floorboards creaked outside the room.

The dollhouse filtered in the natural sunlight from the bedroom window. The tiny open spaces and crevices glowing the soft yellow of the rising afternoon. It illuminated the figure making its way through the house until the tiny toy stopped at a bedroom door.

Slowly the knob turned, and the squeak of the door

opening filled the silence. The Dogman peg hopped inside as the heavy footfalls of its counterpart stepped through the doorway.

Tap! Tap! Tap!

The Dogman paused, cocking his large copper head as it listened to the movements beside him. It stepped to the side, closing the door slightly and peering down at the two human pegs moving forward.

Its large amber eyes took in the scene carefully. Four inches from the wall and curving in their path towards the corner of the room. The beast's lips peeled over its sharp teeth in a vicious smile.

Tap! Tap! Tap!

They were getting closer. But it was faster than their tiny legs could take them. The beast threw its head back and let loose a long, haunting howl.

The hunt was on. The Dogman was coming.

The prey didn't stand a chance.

***

IT WAS a tight fit through the underground tunnels. The sides pressed in on their shoulders and the ceiling was too low to stand straight up. With the light of their cellphones, they illuminated a few feet in front of them before it was swallowed by the expansive darkness. Rey took the lead and whispered back warnings of rocks and uneven ground. In the total silence, they dared not to make more noise than necessary, for fear of waking whatever may be lurking around the next corner.

A cool, damp breeze ran through the tunnels, drawing a shiver from Felicia who instantly regretted not bringing a jacket. But who could have guessed that their journey would take them underground? The musty smell cloyed her nose while they followed the curve in the tunnel towards a soft dripping noise.

A deep body ache settled into their muscles as the ceiling seemed to dip even lower. Rey shifted into a crouch, carefully and slowly shuffling forward with a prayer that the day would end soon.

The darkness eased into a gray tone, the air gained a subtle undertone of plants and wildlife. Another curve in the path revealed the end of the tunnel, illuminated brightly by the sun in an almost blinding fashion. Rey let out a breath he hadn't realized he had been holding as he inched closer to sweet freedom.

"Finally," he grumbled, blinking against the harsh sudden light. They filed out into the quiet and lush forest. The canopy of trees above them swayed gently as the breeze picked up, the branches rustling as they moved back and forth.

Everyone took the moment to stretch their backs and protesting muscles.

"What a fantastic waste of time. At this rate, we'll never find Malora. We need a new plan," Rey huffed.

"Yeah, otherwise we're going to get lost and stuck out here in the dark," Felicia agreed, sitting down on the soft grass and sliding the straps of the backpack off her shoulders.

Laura took in the thick trees that climbed up with the hilly landscape. More cave entrances dotted the area as far as she could see. Many were collapsed shortly after the mouth or too small to squeeze into, adding to the growing sense of frustration.

"We can't give up this far into it," she muttered with a frown.

"I'm not saying we should quit, but we need a better idea of what we're doing before we keep pushing forward. Felicia is right, we could end up hopelessly lost while wandering around out here," Rey pointed out.

A piercing howl rent the air.

"Should we run?" Felicia whispered as she swung the bag back onto her shoulder and clambered to her feet.

"Run where?" Laura inquired in a hoarse whisper.

Rey's jaw clenched and his grip on the gun at his side tightened.

"If we're going to finish this, then we need to go after that sound."

His eyes roamed over his wife and Laura, their gazes a mix of fear and determination. He licked his lip and added, "We need to split up. I'll go first and distract the Dogman when we find him, then you two work on getting that tombstone into the ground. Don't try to find me when you're done. We're going to meet back at the house."

Rey paused to let his words sink in and at his wife's panicked gaze added, "Don't worry. We will all see each other again. But if things get too hairy, abandon the stone and run. We'll figure something else out later."

Laura watched as the couple embraced and exchanged a kiss. They murmured sweet nothings to one another as her throat constricted. If things got too bad, she decided coldly, then she would make sure that Felicia got out safely. No matter what, the Ramseys were going to get home.

And maybe she would get to see Aaron again.

CHAPTER TWENTY-NINE

EACH SNAP of twigs and crunch of leaves under the soles of his feet sent a shiver down Rey's spine. His eyes flitted back and forth between the trees as he moved forward. The bushes were investigated. The cave mouths were peered into.

He knew that at any moment he would meet the beast again. His only relief was knowing his wife and Laura would be far behind him and wouldn't have to deal with the outcome of this fight. He would do it alone and hope what bullets he had were enough.

More branches snapped around him causing his breath to hitch. Was that the creature or more rabbits? His wife or something more sinister?

A low growl accompanied the sound, drawing him to the right. He stooped lower to the ground, watching his step carefully while scouring the woods for the threat. Nothing looked out of the ordinary, but the feeling of being watched haunted him.

Rey flipped the safety off and cocked the gun. He licked his dry lips while shifting around another wide trunk of a tree. Through the thick, overgrown bush ahead was a small clearing at the base of a towering hill. He noted another tunnel in the ground a few feet away from a cave carved into the base of the sloped land.

So which way did the Dogman go?

Rey crouched behind a bush and eyed the area carefully. It was empty save for wildflowers and one massive paw print pressed into the soft ground. It pointed towards the new tunnel.

"I really don't want to face this thing underground," he mumbled to himself, scrubbing a hand down his face. He had unclipped the walkie-talkie from his belt and hovered his finger over the talk button when the Dogman finally emerged.

The creature stepped out of the tunnel and straightened himself to his full height. The muscles in his torso rippling as his shoulders moved back. The large amber eyes of the beast roamed over the empty clearing as he took one step forward. Then another. Suddenly the creature stopped and lifted his large black nose to the air. His chest expanded as he drew in a deep breath, his nose twitching slightly. The Dogman let out a low, vibrating growl as he leaned forward and sniffed again.

Rey's hands shook as he stared into the mix of

canine and human features of the thing standing only ten feet away. Sweat dripped down his back as those long, lean muscles twitched with anticipation. The head almost resembled a large dog, like a golden retriever or something related. The fur was thick and shaggy around its face but thinned and shortened around its throat and collarbones. The slightly curved chest had bare spots, revealing smooth dark skin underneath.

Those calculating and blood thirsty eyes swung around and stared straight at him. The bush may as well have been transparent from the look of hunger that overtook the Dogman. His lips peeled back to reveal rows of razor-sharp teeth, glistening with thick saliva.

Rey's heart shuddered before slamming against his rib cage. Waves of fresh terrors washed over his body, numbing his limbs. The shake grew harder as the Dogman took one prowling step closer. That deep growling growing in its chest.

Then a branch snapped in the distance and the Dogman whipped his head around to face the new intruder. Rey learned what real fear felt like in that moment as he caught the barest glimpse of his wife's long ponytail fluttering behind a tree several yards back.

The Dogman gave him an appraising look before hunching over and launching himself into the forest— heading straight for his true love.

Rey didn't think as he raised the gun and fired off a round. The sound was deafening as the bullet ripped through the barrel and embedded itself in the side of the creature, knocking it off its course.

Screaming a battle cry, Rey pushed himself straight off and squeezed the trigger again and again. The vibrations climbed through his arm as two more bullets went whizzing through the air. The Dogman's enraged snarl shook the area as he spun around to face Rey.

"That's right, asshole, I'm over here," he growled before turning on his heels and running as fast as he could away from the clearing.

His shoes pounded the dirt as his lung burned with the sudden exertion. He heard the ripping and snarling beast behind him but didn't dare to glance back. His eyes remained focused on the trees ahead. Ducking around branches and weaving through obstructions, Rey pushed himself with an icy course of fear pumping in his veins.

Something crashed to his left, and out of the corner of his eye he could see the long, hooked claws of the Dogman's hand swiping at him. Rey threw himself to the left to avoid it, losing his footing in the process. He slammed into the ground and rolled back onto his feet. Catching a glimpse of the massive creature towering over him like he was nothing more than a bug.

Again, it snarled and swung its long arm down as Rey pushed himself forward and darted back through the forest. The claws connected with the packed dirt and grass, slicing through the ground and digging in as it pulled itself closer to its prey.

Rey pumped his legs as hard as he could. He had to get away. He had to live to see tomorrow. He had to make sure the creature never went near his family again. His mind whirled with grotesque images of his bloody death, and that of the ones he loved.

Something hard slammed into his back, forcing him face-first into the dirt. Rey cried out as his jaw hit a protruding root. The metallic taste of blood seeped into his mouth. His head spun for a moment as he rolled over to face the Dogman, leaning over his limp body.

The massive jaws of the beast opened and let out a howl of victory.

Rey's fingers tightened back on the gun still in his grip, but the beast slammed one long hand down, snapping the bones in his upper right arm and forcing him to drop the weapon. The claws dug into his flesh. Rivers of blood rolled out from the wounds and dripped down onto the grass beneath him.

The pain was blinding. It consumed nearly every conscious thought expect for the cold, hard realization that he was going to die.

The Dogman hunched down and opened his fearful, gaping maw. And it was in this moment that a manic bubble of laughter broke through Rey. He realized as the creature loomed closer and the foul stench of its breath wafted over him, that he never actually saw the telltale signs this creature was male. Surely, it would have been pretty big and obvious, right?

Humans couldn't hide it . . . But dogs could . . .

Couldn't they?

"What the fuck are you?" he asked right as the teeth came down and buried in his malleable flesh.

CHAPTER THIRTY

FELICIA CHOKED back a sob as she watched her husband sprint away with the Dogman close on his heels. Tree branches and bark flew out behind the creature as his claws slashed away anything in its path. She stood there stunned until they disappeared.

Laura touched her shoulder gently, offering a small watery smile.

"Don't let what he is doing be in vain. Let's go find Malora and finish this," she murmured.

Felicia swallowed hard and nodded. Together they made their way through the overgrowth into the clearing the Dogman had stood in only minutes before. Without the threat of death looming over their heads, it was almost peaceful. The wind was warm and caressed them as they looked over the area. Small white wildflowers peppered the ground. A deep cave had formed inside of the mountain with a tunnel entrance dipping down into the ground a few feet away.

They looked between the two entrances uncertainly. Felicia nibbled her bottom lip while hitching up the bag that seemed to weigh more now than ever.

Laura nodded towards the cave, pulling out her phone to click on the light as they walked up to the large door. The space was massive—large enough for the Dogman to fit inside and still have plenty of room above its head. The back of the area curved like a half circle and was encompassed by shadows. The air had a slight chill to it as they delved deeper, roaming the flashlight over a few piles of small bones near the walls.

In the far back lay a blanket so deteriorated that Felicia thought a simple sneeze would blow it away. Still, this worn out, grayed fabric lay over something small. The women exchanged a look with one another before Felicia took the brave step forward and nudged the fabric aside.

A spider danced out, darting over her fingers before disappearing into the shadows. Felicia let out a yip and withdrew her hand, shaking it violently as the tiny legs of the insect lingered on her flesh.

"Are you okay?" Laura asked, her voice thick with amusement.

Felicia scowled down at the bundle of fabric with a short nod. Carefully taking one of the edges of the material in her hand, she tossed in open then gasped and fell back.

Nestled inside was a brittle and cracked jawbone

and a small pile of teeth.

Laura let out a shuttering breath as the light wavered in her hand.

"I thought she would have been buried," she whispered.

Felicia nodded, unable to find her voice. The objects looked delicate, as if they would crumble away under the their intent gazes. Felicia finally pulled herself away, climbing to her feet and dusting her hands off on her jeans as she stared back out towards the clearing.

"Okay," she sighed tiredly. "Okay. We found her. Now we just need to give her a proper burial."

"How do you want to do this?" Laura asked quietly.

Felicia walked out of the cave and back into the afternoon light. She didn't have time to overthink the job. Rey was out there battling a beast nearly twice his size and weight. They needed to move.

She slid the bag off her shoulders, leaning it against the bottom of the hill by the mouth of the cave. She unzipped the middle pouch and rooted inside for the hand shovel. As she pulled the tool free, Laura stepped out and stood near her. They decided to make the grave close to the cave. That way they didn't have to carry what was left of the body very far.

Felicia plunged the shovel into the earth and pulled up clumps of dirt as quickly as she could. The hardpacked dirt slowed her progress but soon she had a hole roughly the size of her head and about half a foot deep made. She started on another hole, this one rectangular to fit the bottom of the stone inside, and shallow.

Laura disappeared, reemerging from the cave with the blanket carefully tucked around the bundle of bones and nestled gently in her arms. She knelt and placed the bundle inside the larger hole, then watched silently as Felicia buried it.

Once the hole was completely covered, Felicia gave the dirt a few good pats to make sure it wouldn't be dug back up. She then stood and dusted off her hands again, shivering as she felt as though they would never be clean again. She moved over to the disposed bag and opened the back of it. Originally it was designed to hold a laptop with two Velcro straps sewn into the middle. But inside was a bunch of flowers, which had been slightly crushed during their journey.

Laura was moving the tombstone into place as Felicia knelt back down and rested the flowers on the freshly dug earth. She licked her lips and looked at the older woman anxiously. Laura merely shrugged and moved over to kneel by her side.

"Malora," Laura started quietly. "Malora, I am so sorry for everything you went through. I can't imagine the fear and pain you had to endure. But your Dogman—your guardian—is running around and hurting . . . killing—" Her voice choked up and she had to paused to clear it.

"He is killing innocent people. I know you didn't mean for this to happen. You just wanted to be safe

192

and protected. You wanted to live a good long life. But it's time to let him go. You haven't been forgotten. We remember you and will continue to remember you for as long as we live. Please, Malora. It's over now. It's time to rest in peace."

They bent their heads and sent up a silent prayer. A soft sigh floated by them as the wind stirred and blew through again. The warm current felt like an embrace as it wrapped around their bodies for a moment, then faded away. A sense of peace and tranquility settled in the clearing and a soft chirp rang out from a branch nearby.

"It's over," Laura breathed out in relief. "Thank God, it is finally over!"

"Not yet—we need to find Rey."

CHAPTER THIRTY-ONE

REY'S HEART pounded a quick staccato beat in his ears as teeth ripped through his shoulder and crunched through his bones. A rush of adrenaline swamped his body as he jerked under the creature above him. His mouth opened in a soundless scream while agony flooded his system.

It was the worst pain of his life, and it wasn't stopping. A deep growl reverberated through his body as the Dogman bit deeper.

Muscle and tendon parted like butter as the creature's canines intruded deeper into his flesh. Blood ran in thick rivulets down his skin, pooling in the grass. Then, just as quickly as it started, it ended. The teeth left his skin, and blinking through the haze of agony, Rey watched as the beast reared back and howled. The sun streamed down from the canopy of trees up above him, highlighting the red streaks in the fur of the

Dogman's chin.

The bright amber eyes of the creature met his own for a moment before the weight was lifted from his body. The Dogman stepped back once. Twice. It felt like cotton had filled his ears, yet he swore he heard a soft whimper emanate from the beast. The large, pointed ears fell back and when Rey blinked again, it had simply vanished.

He's gone?

Rey swallowed thickly as he shifted his head to look left and right for any sign of the monster, but nothing was around. He was alone. Relief hit him hard as his body relaxed in the soft grass.

The Dogman was finally gone.

Pushing past the urge to sleep, Rey jerked his good arm closer to his body. It felt laden with lead as he attempted to flex his fingers and find his cellphone. It took a moment, but time was quickly losing any meaning, anyway. His train of thought was quickly fleeing under the weight of the pain. He swallowed again and doubled down on his focus until his fingers brushed over the cool plastic of his cellphone case.

He gingerly lifted it from his pocket and pulled it in front of his face. His eyes squinted as the screen blurred while he drew up his contact list. The service probably wasn't good, but he had to do something. A numbness was seeping in and the wavering images around him weren't settling. He squinted again, noting the bars blinking in and out at the top of the screen while thumbing through until Felicia's name popped up on the short list of contacts.

His hand shook as he tried to press her picture, but he missed and selected a different contact. Rey couldn't even muster a groan of despair; everything was shifting and spinning around him. He typed out *Help* and pressed send before dropping his arm to the side and losing the device to the . . . the . . .

He couldn't think anymore. His breathing was labored as the need to sleep pressed against his eyes. They felt heavy. Everything felt heavy. Everything hurt.

"He said to go back to the house!"

Rey tried to open his eyes, wondering briefly when he had closed them. Something was crashing through the trees towards him. Did he call for help? Who was that?

"He's my husband! He knows I only listen to him half of the time, anyway. We're going to find him!"

Felicia, Rey mused with a small, painful smile. Branches broke and something rustled near him. The sounds filtered in muffled by cotton. Where did he get cotton from? Where was he?

Swimming in an endless ink-black sea, his thoughts drifted past with the churning waves. Something hurt. Everything hurt.

"Over here!" Someone gasped.

He wanted it to stop. He felt nauseous and the pain, oh, the pain was unbearable. It had overtaken his being.

Even breathing hurt. Was he breathing?

"Oh Rey! No!" someone screamed. It sounded so far away, but then something brushed against his arm. The touch was so light and quick he wondered if he had imagined it. Someone was screaming still. Endlessly screaming nonsense.

"Call . . . Help me! We . . . Hurry . . . Stay . . . Me," that voice begged. It was so familiar. It filled his heart with warmth and lifted part of that heavy rock from his soul. He knew that voice. He loved it. He hoped they knew that because it was getting harder and harder to hang on.

". . . no service . . . we . . . carry him . . . I . . . more bars . . ." another voice replied sullenly.

The waves around him churned again and when a large curl of water rose, he released the urge to fight in and sunk further beneath the surface.

Felicia, Sierra, he thought as the pain finally ebbed away.

I'm sorry . . .

CHAPTER THIRTY-TWO

HANK PULLED out his old, gray flip phone and checked his messages for the third time that morning. Normally he hated text messages. They were impersonal, and quite frankly, he didn't understand why someone couldn't simply call to say what they needed to say. It was faster and less frustrating. It was the way it should be.

His granddaughter had tried to convince him otherwise, bless her. She called it an instant letter. Instead of waiting on the post, these messages were delivered instantly to their phones. He got it—really, he did—he just didn't like it and grumbled whenever she insisted on talking to him through them only. But it did give him pictures of the beautiful young woman she was growing up into. And pictures of his son and his wife. The dog named after his wife, Patty.

Today, however, he received a text message that he

didn't know what to do with. He was relieved to be included, and yet worried about what was happening to the poor folks it came from.

We're heading into the forest. – Rey

It had been a few hours now since that message arrived and it had his nerves standing on end. The store being empty didn't help. Now that it was getting colder, nobody was doing improvements on their homes. It would be slow until the weather warmed up again. But he didn't close unless he was out of town visiting his son, which had become less often over the years. Since his wife died, he didn't know what to do with himself. Working was the only meaningful way to pass the time. Now his back ached daily and he was considering hiring some help. Lifting the heavy parts was nearly impossible. Getting out to do the small repairs for the folks around town was too hard to manage some days.

It was almost time to retire. Or step back a little bit. He certainly wished he had someone he could turn to when his mind was wandering like today. He drummed his fingers on the counter that he had wiped down three times since 8:00 am. A restlessness wove through him as the minutes slowly ticked by. He wished he had pressed harder to go with them and help. He didn't know what exactly he could do, but it would have been better than toiling around the shop all morning with a thumb up his ass.

His eyes drifted to the small clock over the doorway again. It was almost noon. It had been nearly three hours since he first got that message. *Didn't they find the grave yet? What happened? Were they in trouble? Were they still alive?* Hank scrubbed a hand down his face while grumbling a string of curses. His fingers toyed over the tiny device, his mind torn and fluttering in all different directions. Should he try texting back or should he wait?

Hank leaned back and grabbed the aged newspaper clipping from under the counter. He smoothed out the wrinkles from the surface and sighed heavily. The Dogman . . . Who would have thought? He hadn't. Not when Laura had first cried about the creature all those years ago when Aaron died. His death shook the small town hard, but everyone chalked her up to a grieving young woman and ignored her pleas for helping in hunting the beast. If only he had taken her seriously . . . Though something about her ramblings did resonate with him. A weird twinge in his gut. It's what made him save the newspaper, and he was thankful he had.

Now a good family was facing the horrors this thing was capable of. They were fighting for their lives, and the lives of everyone who would live in that house after them. Hank never dismissed a funny feeling he got—even if he didn't necessarily act on it right away. His feelings never lied. Which was why he carefully tucked the paper into the breast pocket of his dark blue sweater and hurried towards the door. He dug the keys out of his pocket as he flipped the sign over to say "closed" and flipped the lights off.

He couldn't wait in his shop any longer. Those nice people needed him, even if they were bent on keeping the fight between them and the beast. His eyes had never borne witness to the Dogman before. He only had a picture of paw prints to conjure an image to accompany the name. In fact, logically it wasn't much to make him have faith that this myth truly had any flesh and blood. But something was out there. Something had killed Aaron in a mass of gore that stumped even the police department. Something made those unholy tracks. Something was toying with his newly acquired . . . friends? Yes, his friends.

Hank paused by the door of his old Toyota and pulled out his phone again. No new messages, and his gut was going crazy. He snapped the phone shut and yanked the rusting front door open. Hank slid into the seat with a grunt and slammed the door shut behind him. The engine whined in protest as he cranked the ignition and started the car.

Hank had no plan as he pulled out onto the road. The address from the news clipping echoed in his mind as he navigated the steady traffic towards Malberry Lane. The pavement turned into gravel as he followed the winding road around. The driveways were almost hidden from the street, save for small nondescript mailboxes on the edges of properties. Hank gritted his teeth and slowed down to a crawl as he scanned the numbers on the side of the boxes.

His phone chirped with a new message. Hank hit

the brakes, glancing back wildly to make sure nobody else was on the road with him before he snatched his phone up and flipped it open. It was from Rey and had only one word in it.

Help.

Hank pounded in the emergency line as he hit the gas and sped down the road. The call quickly connected as the numbers flew by in nearly a blur.

"911, what's your emergency?" a woman asked with a monotone voice.

He wedged the device between his shoulder and cheek as he gritted out, "My friend has been in an accident. He needs help right away. Send an ambulance!"

"Sir, what is the address your friend is at?"

"8893 Malberry Lane. He's in the forest behind the house and was attacked by an animal, please hurry!" He jerked the steering wheel and slammed on the brakes as he nearly missed the driveway of the house in question. The dirt path was narrow and pulled a curse from him as he carefully maneuvered around a tree.

"Are you with your friend now?"

"No, but I'll be there faster than you," Hank barked as Laura's old pickup came into view around the bend of the driveway. He steered the car for the U-shaped drive and pulled in front of the door to stay out of the way of the first responders.

"Where are you now?" the lady asked with an edge of concern in her voice.

"I'm at the house now," he replied absently as he

turned the car off and threw the door open.

"Sir, please remain where you are. Help is on the way. Are you able to stay on the phone until they arrive?"

Sirens wailed in the distance, bringing a small bloom of hope to his pounding heart. Still, Hank pushed himself out of the car and kicked the door shut behind him. He started towards the backyard with long, purposeful strides. He passed the built-in garage with barely a glance towards it. The grass came into view, slightly overgrown with two torn up tracks slicing through it.

"Sir?"

"I'm still here, but I ain't waitin' around for y'all to show up," he grumbled into the receiver.

The truck Rey usually drove around was parked sideways with a severed deer head through the front windshield. The sight gave Hank a slight pause before he grumbled under his breath and continued forward. At least it gave credence to his claim of an animal attack, though he wasn't sure how the police would respond when they showed up. Honestly, he was guessing at what happened from a single text. His gut insisted that it was bad, whatever it was. He wasn't one to knock a bad feeling, and it was growing like a heavy stone in his stomach with each step he took into the thick of the trees. Brush, sticks, and tall grass had been crushed in a long path that he followed with the wail of sirens behind him. His cellphone chirped with the rising voice of the call center lady by his side in his clenched fist.

The rising hills littered with entrances for holes, man-made and animal dug, slowly crested and with it, a female sob. His heart stuttered as relief and dread crashed through him. Hank tore through the low-hanging tree branches and overgrown bushes until he finally saw them on the horizon.

Felicia and Laura were ambling through the forest half-dragging a heavy body between them. Rey's head was down, and a steady stream of blood soaked the ground they stumbled over. The women's tear-stained faces would be forever burned into his memory as he ran to aid them. It looked like the poor man had been mauled to death, but the slight rise and fall of his chest belittled the sight. He was alive, if just barely. Words tumbled from Felicia's mouth, but they didn't make any sense to him.

The important thing was Rey was still with them, and help was on the way. Boots pounded the ground in the distance with the bark of a dog leading the team. Carefully, they moved Rey to Hank's shoulder to free Laura from his weight and rushed towards the sound.

"Over here! We're over here!" she screamed, darting ahead of the two with her arms waving over her head.

Hank's legs wobbled when the faces of the search and rescue team came into view. He looked over at Felicia and offered her a watery smile. He wasn't a man who cried easily, but this time, the tears flowed freely down his face.

Everything was going to be okay.

EPILOGUE

FELICIA CRINGED as the men lugged the dollhouse through the trapdoor to the attic. Her hands were clasped tightly by her mouth as the sides of the structure banged against the narrow opening upstairs. Gods, she hoped unconsciously the door would still close after they were through. One of the fellows, a man named Roger, grunted from the top of the landing as he pulled the house the rest of the way onto the wooden floor above. The sounds of wood grating against wood trailed down to her as they dragged it further into the small space.

"You sure you want this in the very back?" he called down, poking his head out of the opening to stare at her curiously, his disheveled blond hair sticking up around his head. She sighed, having thought the job would not have been this difficult. But the entire time from dragging the house out of Sierra's room up to the attic had been filled with the young men bumping into things, knocking the edges of the house against corners, and nearly slipping on the carpeted steps up to the office room. Honestly, she should have waited until Rey was out of the hospital to get the job done. But she wanted every reminder of the creature gone. Hidden away from her sight, and hopefully, resting eternally as a dark secret of the Ramsey family.

Sierra didn't seem to have many memories regarding the beast. She missed him outside of the window when he had attacked, thankfully. And the nightmares that had plagued her weeks ago seemed to have stopped. But Felicia didn't want to leave reminders around to trigger them again. Sierra was young; more than likely she would forget about this event as she grew older. Only her parents had to remember the Dogman and what destruction he had brought to their lives.

As far as her daughter knew—and the rest of the town for that matter—Daddy had been attacked by an animal in the woods. And he was in the hospital recovering. Monique was with her right now, while Felicia got the house in order. It had been four days, and Rey was awake enough to complain endlessly about having to be admitted. But the wounds had been deep and required surgery to fix. He would still be tied to the bed for another few days.

Then hopefully everything could go back to normal. They would never have to deal with this again.

"Yeah, and please be careful," she called back.

Roger nodded with a roguish grin. "Don't worry, ma'am. We always are," he added with a cheeky wink that made her roll her eyes with a groan.

Whatever. They were recommended by Hank to work quickly and cheaply, which admittedly, they did. The same day she had called them about moving some furniture, they had arrived within a few hours and started without any questions. All for ten dollars.

It was a good deal and once the ruckus upstairs stopped, Felicia let out a sigh of relief. For the first time, she felt a wave of peace settle over her. She only had a few more things to take care of and then she could go back to her family.

When the men came down and locked the trapdoor back up, she paid them and thanked them for the help. Roger smiled and tipped his head, offering to come again if she ever needed anything. Felicia wrinkled her nose but stood politely by the door until finally they stepped out and headed for their beat-up white minivan.

She watched as the vehicle rumbled to life and eased out of the driveway before turning towards the bedroom. Inside, she ventured for the bed, sitting on the edge by a small wooden nightstand with a white lamp resting on top. She took a steadying breath before pulling the single drawer open and pulling out the black diary and a pen. The book contained some of Malora Hail's life, an innocent woman who turned into a vengeful spirit, and the details of the lives of the homeowners before them. Some of the recollections ended well enough, while others unfortunately ended too soon.

The binding cracked as Felicia flipped through the aged and worn pages to an empty space. She shifted on the rose-colored duvet as she poised the pen over the unmarked sheet of paper. It needed to be updated. The end to a horrifying tale.

September 3rd, 2007

It is hard to image what normal is, and whether or not it'll come back to us. We have seen and experienced things very few would believe. In the beginning of August, we moved into this house. We thought it would be the start to a better life. In the pictures online it looked like a dream come true. It turned into a nightmare that held us captive for nearly a month. But within the darkness we found a stronger love for one another, new friends that will last a lifetime, and the hope to keep pushing forward. The land was tormented by a beast known as the Dogman. This is how we finally broke the curse and won our freedom . . .

Hours later she closed the book and slowly stood up. Her hand cramped from jotting down the miraculous tale. It would be immortalized on paper from here on out. A reminder of all that they had survived, and the relief they had in knowing no one else would have to face the same fate.

The sun was setting outside, illuminating the room in a dusty orange glow as she made her way back out into the hall. The book was complete, and so it would return to where it had been found. Safe and sound. She cracked open the trapdoor and carefully lowered the sliding ladder down. The attic was dusty and dark, but back near the only window in the tiny space was the beautiful old desk with the secret drawer. She carefully stepped around the growing pile of boxes and pulled the old drawer open. It only took a moment to locate the drop-down ceiling and hide the leather tome away.

The floorboards creaked softly under her feet as she retreated to the door, pausing only to text Monique and let her know she was heading back to the hospital. The door groaned as it closed and latched behind her, pitching the attic back in darkness. A soft scratching disturbed the silence, emanating from the old desk. Deep inside of it the black book rustled. The spine bent with a groan, and the pages flipped with a crinkle. The dark ink on the page faded and shifted, the words rearranging carefully. The scrawling handwriting changed into stark and angry slashes.

July the 25th

He spat out a vile, evil curse as he walked away. By the weeks end I must become his bride and except the consequences of striking him or He promises more than death. He promises annihilation. And neither man nor animal would see my face. Not tree, stone, nor wind would whisper my name. My soul will blink out before reaching the Heavens.

And I believe him.

I must do something about this. I do not want to be forgotten. I do not want to die. I WILL LIVE.

AUTHOR'S NOTE

Thank you for reading Hunted. This has been an interesting story to write. The original inspiration came to me when I was at the bookstore and saw a picture of a creepy looking dollhouse. The image stuck in my mind for weeks, and I decided that I had to write something featuring a dollhouse that was possessed or cursed—something that did that picture justice. I wish I had bought the picture, but when I went back it wasn't on the shelf. Hindsight sucks.

The entire plotline didn't develop until months later, but I explored a dozen different ideas with my family off and on during that time. They're awesome. Everyone bounced theories with me and listened patiently as I rambled for hours about this family who was being haunted by a ghost or something. Then finally I stumbled across an article about the Dogman of Michigan and the whole picture came together. I knew instantly what I wanted to do and started writing it out that night. Thank you, again, to my super awesome family who helped me talk the details out and get that plan down.

The Dogman of Michigan is this creature the roams our forests with the head of a dog but the torso of a man. It walks on two legs and is said to be intelligent. Honestly, I took the lore and smashed it half a dozen ways to Sunday for this book, but the bones of it are still there. I was able to also mix in some other lore from Arizona (to create my dollhouse dolls) and was inspired by a few different ghost stories I've heard over the years.

This book is a mishmash of inspiration that has been fun to explore and write out. Honestly, it might be my favorite book so far.

ABOUT THE AUTHOR

C.R. Garmen developed her passion for writing at a young age. Starting with retelling the story of three little pigs, she went on to dream of being an author one day. Born and raised in the suburbs of Detroit, she is very close to her family, especially her younger siblings who light up her world and continue to support and fuel her passion for telling stories. Jack of all trades, master of none; C.R. Garmen dabbles in every genre, finding that each one is just a new challenge to explore and take on.

Follow her on Facebook for more updates about new releases.

WWW.FACEBOOK.COM/CRGARMEN

And check out her blog for some exclusive interviews, new releases, and more!

WWW.CRGARMEN.WORDPRESS.COM

www.ingramcontent.com/pod-product-compliance
Lightning Source LLC
Chambersburg PA
CBHW031328170626
46807CB00002B/614